DEADLY LIES
AND
DOG-EARED SECRETS

WHISKEY MYSTERY #6

In Your Face Ink LLC
9524 W. Camelback Road
#130-182
Glendale, AZ 85305
www.inyourfaceink.com
www.whiskeydogmysteries.com

First printed in the United States of America by In Your Face Ink LLC

ISBN 979-8-9924943-9-6 (hardback)
ISBN 979-8-9934752-0-2 paperback)
ISBN 979-8-9934752-1-9 (e-book)

Book design and cover by Rick Schank of Purple Couch Creative

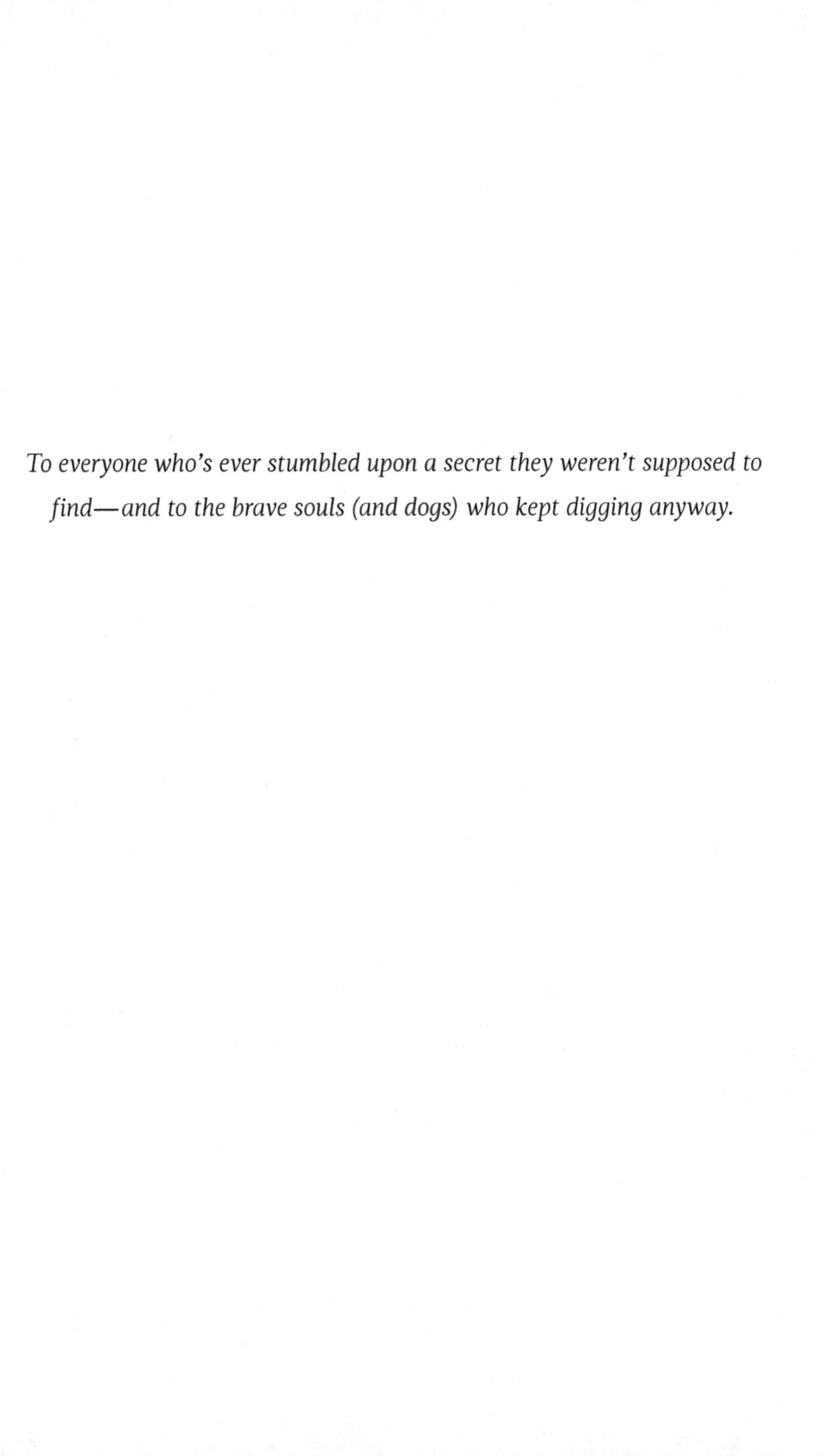

To everyone who's ever stumbled upon a secret they weren't supposed to find—and to the brave souls (and dogs) who kept digging anyway.

THE BROKEN SPINE

CHAPTER 1

The green door of Carter's Canine Coiffure opened, letting in a crisp gust of late October air scented with dry leaves and woodsmoke. Red-haired Sarah Carter, age twenty-eight, barely looked up from the Australian red heeler cattle dog in her stainless steel tub. Her hands were buried in a mountain of soap suds that clung to Whiskey's rough but soft coat like clouds around the Mt. Everest's peak.

"*Bonjour,*" Sarah called to Daphne Smith, a well-dressed and eccentric woman who spoke mostly French, though she had lived in Cottageville, Iowa, her whole life and had never traveled to Quebec, Montreal, or Paris, or anywhere where the language was native.

Daphne wore a black cashmere turtleneck sweater over burnt orange pants tucked into black riding boots. She carried her costume-wearing buff colored French bulldog Pierre, who was dressed as a bee and looking none too happy about it, under her arm like a football.

Twenty-year-old Emily Colt, Sarah's assistant groomer and close friend, stepped forward to the counter. "*Bonjour,* Daphne. *Bonjour,* Pierre. You make a cute bee." She reached out her hand and scratched between his ears.

"*Nous sommes en crise. Pierre s'est cassé un ongle. Il faut le réparer.*" Daphne used her hands to spread the toes on Pierre's front left foot. One toenail was barely hanging on. Fortunately for the dog and for Emily, it hadn't broken to the quick. And though Em didn't speak French, she understood what Daphne was showing her. One fast snip and the problem was solved.

"*Tu es une bouée de sauvetage.*" Daphne patted Emily's hand, threw a twenty on the counter, and then walked out the door.

"If it was all that easy," Emily said to Sarah.

"Well done," Sarah said, rinsing Whiskey until the water ran clear. Whiskey didn't require many baths, maybe one or two a year. Cattle dogs tended to stay clean and rarely stank. Their double coat and natural grooming abilities kept them mostly clean and dry. Case in point being how Whiskey bit his own toenails and scratched them against pavement when they needed to be trimmed or worn down. He hated Sarah to get anywhere near him with the clippers, and he had been that way since he was a pup, seven years ago.

When Sarah shut off the water, Whiskey gave a happy shake, sending droplets flying across the room. Emily squealed in delight, her rosy painted cheeks bunching toward her eyes. Emily often dressed edgy and often in black, but today she surprised Sarah by coming to work wearing a blue and white gingham pinafore over a white blouse. She had extensions in her hair that were bowed with the same blue and white gingham into two ponytails, one down each side of her face and dress front.

"Dorothy?" Sarah had asked, her eyebrows raised in surprise.

"Iconic," Em said.

Sarah planned to change into her costume when they were done with work for the day. This afternoon was the annual Halloween Pet Parade, and Sarah was so grateful the city council and mayor's office took charge of it. Sarah and Emily had already organized one Cottageville Pet Parade this year for Valentine's Day, and while it had been a huge hit, it was more work and responsibility than Sarah wanted. The last few months she had been more focused on her personal life, including boyfriend Jared Greene's exhibit at a gallery in Prague. Sarah flew there with him for the opening while Emily housesat and Whiskey-sat and ran the Coiffure single handedly. And she did a fabulous job.

"Come on, Whisk," Emily said, leading the dog to a grooming table. He needed a good brushing and a blow dry so that he'd be ready for his costume.

"I can't believe he'll wear a hat for you," Em said as she ran the brush along his spine.

He looked at her and moved his black lips into a grin.

"Well, the collared tweed cape looks dumb without it," Sarah said, picking up a brush and starting on Whiskey's right side.

"But he hates hats," Em insisted. "And besides, calling you Sarahlock Holmes is starting to catch on around town. So shouldn't Whiskey be dressed as Watson instead of Sherlock?"

"Maybe. But I'm not really sure what Watson wore." Sarah glanced out their front window. They were half a block from Main Street, and the whole area was humming with activity. The Halloween Pet Parade had become a beloved tradition in their town, drawing families, tourists, and every canine and human companion with a festive bone in their bodies.

By mid-morning, the sidewalks were lined with hay bales and pumpkins. Black and orange streamers fluttered from the lampposts, and Cottageville Park, the endpoint of the parade, was filled with booths selling apple cider, pumpkin bars, and homemade dog treats shaped like ghosts and jack-o-lanterns. Java and Juice, which was owned by Sarah's BFF Ginger Jones and where Sarah's boyfriend worked part-time as a barista, always had the most popular booth. People stood in line a dozen deep to purchase the caramel apple scones, candied ginger rolls, and cinnamon apple tarts. The cafe had closed early to open their makeshift store at the park.

Sarah had put a table next to the Java and Juice booth, though she and Em wouldn't staff it until after the parade. They were offering free pawdicures and candy corn printed bandanas, and in the early morning, they had put up signage and organized treat samples, with obsessive precision.

And now that Whiskey was slightly damp but perfectly fluffed, Sarah attached his Sherlock collared cape and secured the hat to the top of his head with the chin strap. He promptly batted the hat with his paw and pulled it off.

"Whiskey," she said, "I thought we had a deal."

He flashed her a black lipped smile and walked to the Coiffure door, leaving the hat on the floor where it fell.

Emily chuckled. "I didn't think he'd wear it for long." She picked it up and moved the towels they had used to the washing machine and threw them in. "Come on, Sarah. I don't want to be late."

Sarah removed the denim dog print apron she was wearing and hung it on a hook. "Hang on a sec," she said, disappearing into the bathroom.

When she emerged, Emily gasped. Her eyes were wide. "No, Sarah. Seriously?" Her grin was bigger than a quokka's.

Sarah was thrilled by Em's reaction to her surprise. Sarah had donned a tweed jacket and hat that matched Whiskey. She wore a white button down shirt and tweed vest over brown pants and oxfords, and she carried a magnifying glass in her hand and had an unlit pipe in her mouth.

"Stand near Whiskey. I need a photo," Emily insisted. "This is awesome."

Sarah hammed it up in a variety of poses: hugging her dog, standing above him with her mouth agape and her index fingers and thumbs pointed like weapons down at him, inspecting him with the magnifying glass, and holding the glass up to one of his eyes.

Emily's chuckles filled the Coiffure as she captured every pose.

"Okay, okay," Sarah said. "We've gotta get going." She locked up her business and doublechecked that Em carried the box with the samples of oatmeal dog shampoo and other treats that they would hand out at their table. They walked up Main Street and headed to the park to finish their set up and to talk to clients new and old and to meet curious out-of-town pet owners. Whiskey was off-leash as usual and led the way like a parade marshal.

Jared was working the Java and Juice booth with Ginger. At one point, while he was serving a customer a cup of cider, he caught Sarah's eye and smiled. She loved his auburn-headed handsomeness, how his green eyes sparkled whenever he looked her way. Sarah's heart did a somersault. They had been a couple for almost a year, but his smiles felt as exciting as the first one he had ever given her many years ago.

The air in the park was filled with barks, laughter, children in capes and fairy wings darting between the stalls and around in circles. An occasional squeaky toy cut through the din, and the scent of baked apples, caramel, and cinnamon mixed with the woodsy notes of fallen leaves. It was the kind of the day that made Sarah feel grounded and whole. Her life in Cottageville hadn't been perfect—and some moments had been downright scary—but events like today's made her grateful for the slower pace and strong community that surrounded her, so much different than in the West Coast city where she grew up.

At three twenty-five, Mayor Trish McGowan, who was back from taking a couple-month sabbatical to attend to some personal things, kicked off the parade over a sound system with a "Happy Halloween, everyone. If you can make your way to the parade start line, we will begin shortly." Sarah and Whiskey raced through a shortcut they knew to get to the south end of Main Street. They hung back so that they were almost at the end of the participants.

Dogs of all shapes and sizes marched with their owners. Princess pugs, pirate retrievers, and one particularly proud schnauzer in a hot dog bun flaunted their stuff and stopped for photos or an occasional treat. Whiskey walked off-leash beside Sarah, trotting like he knew how good he looked...even with the hat he hated. Spectators laughed and pointed at them and some of the locals cheered at their costumes. Children waved from the sidewalks and Sarah waved in return.

They passed the town library, decorated at its entrance with dangling paper bats. Sarah waved to Carole Binds, the head librarian, who was handing out bookmarks and candy to anyone with only two legs under four feet tall.

Then, as they reached the entrance to the park near a big scarecrow display, Whiskey stopped in his tracks. His ears were rigid. He sniffed the air.

"What is it, boy?" Sarah asked, tugging gently on his collar. There weren't many people behind them, but Sarah didn't want them holding up the parade.

But Whiskey wouldn't budge. His whole body was stiff.

Then he barked—sharp and low—and bolted forward, dragging Sarah who still had a hold of his collar, toward the corn stalks and bales of hay that surrounded the biggest scarecrow in the center of the display.

Sarah stumbled, catching her balance just as Whiskey stopped in front of the scarecrow's feet.

"Whiskey, stop. You're going to—"

But the words died in her throat.

Whiskey had his paws on something that wasn't straw. Something pale and motionless, half-hidden behind a pumpkin.

Sarah blinked.

But the thing didn't change or move.

It was a hand.

A real, human hand.

Her stomach lurched.

She pulled her phone from her pocket and called Police Chief James Order. After all of the mysteries she had stumbled across in the last two years, she had him on speed dial. "Come quickly to the park entrance," she said, "to the big scarecrow display. Whiskey found someone and they aren't moving."

She disconnected and moved closer. Sarah pushed aside the corn husks and hay. What she uncovered made her gasp.

There, beneath the big scarecrow lay a man dressed in a costume nearly identical to the big scarecrow. He wore a brown jacket, a plaid shirt, and had straw stuffed in his sleeves. Only he wasn't part of the official display. He was human. And he was dead.

Sarah swallowed hard and looked at the man's face. His head was lolled to the side at an unnatural angle. His skin was pale, his lips tinged blue. And though Sarah didn't know him well, she recognized him. Paul Whitmore.

He was new to Cottageville and kept to himself. He had moved into Micas Brighton's house after Micas's death when his daughter Lottie—who lived in Los Angeles—decided to keep the house and rent it out.

Whiskey sat beside Paul's body, calm but alert, as if he was guarding the scene.

Sarah knelt beside her dog and put her fingers against Paul's wrist, seeing if he was warm or cold.

She didn't realize the parade had stopped behind her and that a crowd was now forming, until she heard Chief James' voice of authority yell, "Coming through. Step aside, people. Let the police through."

Sarah didn't move. Her heart was pounding. Questions flooded her brain: *Why had Paul moved here? Why was he dressed like a scarecrow? He didn't have a pet in the parade. Who would want him dead?*

She looked up at the scarecrow looming above them. It had a pumpkin head with a crooked painted grin.

But that grin no longer looked cheerful.

Chief James greeted Sarah and checked the body. His officers had people step back and they put up yellow tape. They secured the perimeter and began taking statements of those in the crowd.

Sarah talked to Officer John Beams and gave her official statement.

Jared came for Sarah and thrust a cup of warm cider into her hands. "You're in shock, sweetie. Drink it." He scratched Whiskey's head. "Good boy. Such a good boy."

Sarah took a sip of the cider. It tasted like cinnamon, apple, and confusion. Her eyes met Jared's. "I can't believe he's dead."

Jared put his arms around her. "I didn't know him well. People said he was quiet, didn't bother anyone."

Sarah frowned. "But someone bothered him. Maybe even enough to dress him like a scarecrow and leave him there. That's not random. That's a message." She shivered.

Emily approached them, her arms wrapped around her chest like she was trying to comfort herself. "Sarah. It's so creepy. Like a

Halloween horror movie. But real." She looked like she might vomit.

"We're going to find out who did this," Sarah whispered to Emily and Jared. She stroked Whiskey's fur with the fingers of her right hand.

Jared sighed. "Sarah, maybe we should let the police handle this one."

But Sarah was already thinking about Paul Whitmore's quiet demeanor. About how Carole Binds had helped him look through the library's archives. Carole said he asked odd questions about the town's history. He had asked her and others about an old photograph he was trying to find.

Sarah's mind spun as leaves skittered across the path at her feet.

Whiskey's ear twitched.

The parade was over.

But something else had just begun. And that started with Sarah's promise to a dead man she barely knew: *I will find your killer. And not just because Whiskey and I are dressed like Sherlock Holmes. But because everyone deserves justice.*

CHAPTER 2

Sarah woke the next morning because Whiskey's cold, wet nose was nuzzling her neck before his long tongue slurped her left cheek. "Okay, dog," she grumbled, "I'm awake."

He hopped off the bed and ran to the door, expecting her to follow.

"Can't I take a moment to pee first?" Sarah took three steps toward the bathroom when Whiskey barked and ran to her then circled her legs, nipping at her calf.

"Okay, okay. You don't need to herd me. I'll go let you out."

He seemed to understand as he raced to the door again. Sarah followed in her flannel cartoon dog pj pants and matching tank top.

Whiskey sat on his haunches at the back door, and as she approached, he pawed the door once to signal his impatience.

"Dog, one day could you return the favor and let me hit the bathroom with the same VIP access I give you?"

Sarah unlocked the door and Whiskey bolted down the stairs into the yard. Sarah's eyes registered a flash of orange and white as Whiskey stormed the fence like a general in battle. "You aren't going to catch him, boy. Mozart's too devious." Mozart lived diagonally across the street with Robert Wise, the music teacher at Cottageville High. The cat's favorite hobby was tormenting the cattle dog, usually by sitting within his sightline and ignoring him by licking himself and giving his nemesis an occasional side eye.

"Do your business or come back inside," Sarah said, watching a brown leaf flutter in the mild breeze before tumbling to the grass.

Whiskey lifted his leg against an azalea before trotting back into the house. As Sarah locked the back door, she heard his metal tags clink against his water bowl. She knew next he'd hit his paw against his food bowl as an attempt to summon his breakfast.

"Coming," she said, before making a pit stop into the hallway bathroom to empty her bladder.

In the kitchen, she dumped a cup of salmon-based grain-free kibble into Whiskey's bowl. She said a silent prayer of thanks that Jared had made a pot of coffee strong enough to wake a ghost and that it was still hot. She poured some into a white mug with a black interior and black writing on the exterior that read "100% chance there's cattle dog hair in here".

Whiskey gave a soft huff that his food bowl was once again empty.

She leaned down and scratched between his ears. "Let me shower and then we'll take a walk. But Whisk, try not to find any bodies today. Okay?" She chuckled to herself at her lame attempt at humor.

He turned his head at an angle eying her, like he was considering her suggestion. But then he raced through the house ahead of her as she carried her coffee toward the bedroom. Whiskey was curled into a ball in the middle of the bed with his eyes shut as she walked through the room and closed the bathroom door.

As the hot water ran over her, Sarah's mind flashed with scenes from yesterday: dogs and children in cute costumes, the pet parade, the smell of cinnamon and pumpkins, the crowds. But her chest tightened as she relived the pale, lifeless hand limp on the straw, the scarecrow that wasn't a scarecrow. Sarah frowned and wondered if the police had any clues.

Even though they had cordoned off the big holiday display with yellow tape, after a cursory investigation, Chief James had asked his officers and the mayor to clear the park. All booths were to be left up, but all people and pets were to evacuate so the police could try to pinpoint the crime scene. Sarah wondered if the technicians had worked through the afternoon and night and if the park had re-opened to the public.

After pulling on jeans and a forest green sweatshirt and putting her hair into a messy bun atop her head, Sarah shoved her feet into sheepskin-lined boots. She pocketed her phone and her keys, grabbed her to-go cup, and she and Whiskey shut and locked their front door. Whiskey stayed with her up the slight hill, past their neighbors' houses on the way to the park.

Robert Wise drove past in his olive green Volkswagen, giving a short blast of his horn as a greeting.

Sarah waved at him, then crossed the street into the park and followed the dirt path. Whiskey led with his nose on an invisible trail through the grass. Halfway through the acreage, she spied the booths, empty of their offerings. All excitement of Halloween had exited when Cottageville's citizens and guests had been evicted from the space. The uninhabited structures reminded Sarah of an Old West ghost town. The lack of people in what was often the main play and picnic area in town was eerie.

On the Chin's Chinese restaurant's booth, one end of a streamer of orange crepe paper jack-o-lanterns had worked its way loose and fluttered in the breeze like a Buddhist prayer flag releasing its blessings. Whiskey chased after it barking. He jumped and tried to catch it between his teeth, but he wasn't quite tall enough to reach.

"Come on, Whisk," Sarah said, leading him to the candy corn printed fabric that covered the Carter's Canine Coiffure table. The boxes of bandanas and treats were right where she left them, hidden by the cloth and stacked underneath near the metal table leg. Yesterday, she had grabbed her zippered case of pawdicure utensils from underneath the table as she and Jared had made their way home, along with all of their neighbors. Today, after their walk, she would return to the park with her CJ and load the table and boxes into the Jeep and take them to the Coiffure. But for now, she led Whiskey past the giant scarecrow and hay bale display and tried not to shudder when the image of Paul Whitmore's hand flashed through her mind.

When they exited the park, Whiskey beelined to the right and up the stairs to his buddy Bill Reid's front porch. Bill was around eighty, a widower who read the newspaper and drank his daily cup of coffee outside year-round, regardless of the weather, claiming he was of hearty Iowaian stock. He kept a gallon glass jar of dog biscuits on the table next to him, and every dog in town dragged their human to see Bill.

"Whiskey, where's your Sherlock hat? Though we both know you don't need that to solve a mystery." Bill's blue-gray eyes sparkled behind his silver glasses.

"Good morning, Bill," Sarah said from the bottom of the steps.

"Good morning, Sarah. How are you today?" Bill unscrewed the top of the jar and reached inside for a biscuit. He commanded Whiskey to sit and give him his paw to shake before he gave the dog the treat.

That made Sarah happy as she preferred for Whiskey to work for his treats. "I'm fine. It's been a quiet morning. The park was deserted."

"Yes, the police wrapped up around midnight, I think. At least that's when they killed all of those floodlights. I felt like I was in an Alaskan summer and couldn't sleep because it was so bright."

"Was it noisy, too?"

"Not with my windows closed."

"Well that's good at least."

"Are you working today?"

"No. It's our Saturday off." The Coiffure was open every other Saturday for the convenience of clients who couldn't make weekday appointments. "The only thing I need to do is pack up our things from the park."

"Good. Good. Are you headed to Java and Juice?" Sarah stopped by her best friend's cafe every work day to get coffee, breakfast pastries, and lunch salads for her and Emily. On weekends, she usually stayed away from the cafe, but today, because of the crime, she was making an exception. J and J was often juicy with gossip, and since the police seemed to be keeping any news on the downlow, Sarah craved the scuttlebutt.

"I think so Bill, a cream cheese filled pumpkin spice muffin and small town rumors sound like the perfect Saturday morning," Sarah jocosely said.

Sarah and Whiskey bid adieu to Bill, who said he may see her at Java and Juice. Sarah and Whiskey crossed over Main Street and walked the half-block to the familiar red doors. The bell chimed overhead, but it was barely heard as the cafe buzzed louder than the espresso machine. Townsfolk clustered at tables, heads bent together like hens in a coop. Mayor Trish McGowan and her best friend Barbara Order, the police chief's wife, usually held court at the first table by the door. But today, they were notably absent. Everyone in the cafe stopped talking at once when they saw Sarah and Whiskey. A few people waved or nodded their heads. The town's paramedics, Walter and Wendy Parks, who sat against the wall called, "Hi, Sarah." A few other people Sarah recognized followed suit.

But Whiskey trotted to the glass cases of food, and Sarah followed him since there was no line for orders. Ginger was behind the counter, her caramel-colored braids bouncing as she poured lattes and passed them to her customers waiting off to the side. Jared, wearing his green barista apron, was at the pastry case, sliding muffins dotted with crystalized ginger and butterscotch chips onto the trays. His face looked pinched, though he smiled through the glass when Whiskey peered in at him from the other side.

"Whiskey, don't put your nose against the glass," Sarah said.

"Morning, Sarahlock." Ginger's voice had a teasing singsong quality to it. She gave a theatrical bow. "Word around town is you solved the case before the parade even finished."

"Ha ha." Sarah felt her cheeks warm. "Hardly. Whiskey found Paul. I just...called it in." Sarah set her to-go cup on the counter.

"Well, people already think you and Whiskey have a sixth sense for trouble." Ginger grinned. Then she dropped her voice, leaned against the counter, and added, "They're also saying Chief James is unhappy that his officers didn't discover the body before you did."

Sarah sighed. "It wasn't like I went looking for it."

"You never do...and yet..." Ginger's voice trailed off. "So, how can I help you investigate? I'll be free around three."

"I don't know," Sarah said. "I keep wondering why Paul. He barely spoke to anyone, I think."

"He was only in here once, maybe twice," Ginger said, sliding Sarah's to-go cup filled with dark roast black coffee across the counter.

Jared handed Sarah a bag containing a cream cheese filled pumpkin spice muffin. He reached across the counter to give Whiskey one of Ginger's homemade chicken dog biscuits. Sarah tapped her credit card against the payment terminal and added a healthy tip.

"Do you know anything about him?" she asked her BFF. "Like heard any gossip about where he was from or why he moved here, of all places?"

"This morning I heard someone say he was looking for someone," Jared said.

Sarah pursed her lips. "Looking for someone or something?"

Jared's ginger eyebrows moved closer together as he thought. "Umm. I'm not sure."

"And there's the usual speculation," Ginger added. "Everything from a mob hit to he was in witness protection and it caught up to him to committing suicide in grand gesture style." Her mouth turned down like she ate something bitter. "People are weird and cruel."

"Cause of death?" Sarah asked. "It looked like his neck was broken, but I don't want to make any assumptions."

"Not officially released, as far as I know," Ginger said. "The Chief, his wife, Beams, Grimes, no one has been in yet today."

"No, because they probably worked late last night," Sarah said.

"Right," Ginger said.

Jared said, "Hey, if you and Whiskey are headed home, I'll walk with you to the park. Ginger wants me to dismantle our booth."

"Yes," Ginger said, "go now while you can. I've got this covered."

Jared pulled his apron string over his head and walked the apron through the double doors into the kitchen. When he returned, he clasped Sarah's hand and entwined their fingers. Whiskey followed them out the door.

CHAPTER 3

"Carole was in earlier this morning," Jared said. "She said Paul came to the library frequently to look at old newspaper archives of *The Cottageville Courier*."

"Really? Did she know what he was looking for?"

"If so, she didn't say."

Sarah made a mental note to stop by the library later in the day.

After three cars passed at the requisite twenty-five mile per hour speed limit in their one traffic light town, they crossed over Main Street and entered the park. Whiskey took off at a trot and Sarah spied his target: Sascha, the German Shepherd who lived with Chief James and Barbara. Sascha looked as if she was doing the 50-yard dash through an open grassy area to the right of the playground. The chief was out of uniform in jeans and a flannel shirt and carrying a Chuckit!, which he used to launch an orange and blue ball. Sascha chased after the ball with Whiskey running at her heels.

Jared dropped Sarah's hand so he could start dismantling Java and Juice's wood-framed booth. "I'll see you at home," she said to Jared, planting a quick kiss on his cheekbone.Then Sarah bypassed her table and walked toward Chief James and the dogs.

"Morning, Sarah."

Sascha dropped the ball at her human's feet, and then she and Whiskey waited like coiled springs to race after it again.

"Hi, Chief. How's it going?" Sarah desired to ask specific questions about what she was sure was a murder, but she doubted Chief James would answer.

"Slow, and I'm tired today."

"I heard you were here at the park until at least midnight," Sarah said as the ball flew through the air and the dogs' paws pounded against the earth in their pursuit.

"We were."

"Do you know if Paul Whitmore has a next of kin? I mean, he was new to town and I never heard anyone mention a spouse or a partner or a kid in conjunction with him."

"We're still working on that." The chief used the lime green Chuckit! launcher to pick up the spit-slicked ball. He held the launcher upright, flicked his wrist, and let the ball sail. The dogs gave chase.

"His neck was at a sickening angle," Sarah remarked.

"It was," Chief James agreed, giving away nothing. "Thank you for finding him."

"Really it was Whiskey." Sarah reached down to rub her dog's ears. After the last run back with Sascha carrying the ball, he had collapsed on the ground at Sarah's feet. His long tongue protruded from his mouth and he panted from the exertion of the chase. Sascha sat at Chief James' feet, eying the ball in the launcher. She was up for another run.

"She never tires of this. Reminds me of you and solving mysteries." Chief James smiled at Sarah. "I know you want to ask me a thousand questions. I appreciate that you aren't. There's not much I can share, not much we know. It's still early..." His voice trailed off and he threw the ball one more time.

Whiskey bolted after his friend, who had a head start.

Sarah's voice was low and gentle like a breeze when she said, "I don't think he was killed where I found him."

Chief James' eyes studied her face for a few moments, his brown eyes boring into hers, before he gazed at the empty playground. "The cause of death has not been confirmed, but why do you think he wasn't killed there?"

"If his broken neck caused his death, he had to have been hung, dragged by his neck, or dropped from a height. I didn't see ligature bruising and he didn't look battered. So it is a simple deduction on my part."

"We are working out the details and awaiting the autopsy and tox screen."

The dogs had returned with the ball, but Sarah and Chief James didn't acknowledge them. Sarah looked back at Jared to see how far along he had gotten on the dismantling of the booth. She saw that Daniel, Ginger's fiancé and owner of Buck and Son Hardware, was now helping him.

"Had you met Paul?" Sarah asked the chief.

"I had heard he moved into Micas Brighton's house, but we hadn't officially been introduced. You?"

"I met him once. He was talking to Bill one morning on Bill's front porch when Whiskey stopped by for his daily treat. He seemed nice, didn't say much. He asked how long I've lived here. I told him I've been coming to Cottageville most of my life visiting my grandmother, Gigi, and that I've lived here since I inherited her house seven years ago. He said something like, 'oh it's nice to get something from family.'" Sarah frowned, thinking how wistful he sounded. *Why was that?*

Her thought was interrupted when Chief James cleared his throat and said, "Sarah, I can't stop you from poking around. I know that. But can you focus your sleuthing on who Paul was and leave the investigation of his death to us? I'd like you to stay out of danger, if that's possible. You've had more stalkers and hate mail these last two years than most people get in a lifetime."

"Now, Chief," Sarah joked, "I have no idea why you'd think I'd put myself in danger." Visions of sloshing through a Dumpster and being threatened too many times to count flashed through her mind and caused her to shiver.

"And if you find out anything, anything at all, about Paul, please let us know. Come on, Sascha, we've got to get home." He clipped a leash to Sascha's harness. "Good seeing you, Sarah. Stay safe, and have a good day. Bye, Whiskey." The chief shoved the Chuckit! stick into his back pocket and led his dog toward the Main Street park exit, greeting Daniel and Jared as he passed them.

Sarah watched them go before urging Whiskey to head toward home. Sarah planned to eat the spiced muffin and drink her second coffee while she searched social media for any accounts or mentions of Paul Whitmore. Surely some site somewhere had to have a record of him.

But as Sarah approached her front door, she had another idea. As soon as it was a decent hour for a phone call to the West Coast, she planned to ring Lottie Brighton and see what she knew about her tenant. Maybe he had provided a previous address or driver's license, or references on his rental application or lease. And then Sarah's heart twinged when she realized her new friend would have to find a new tenant.

Sarah hoped the house wasn't the crime scene. Lottie didn't need to go through that again—both the physical cleaning of the place and the emotional and mental anguish. At least, Sarah thought, Iowa was one of the few states where homeowners didn't have to disclose a death when selling or renting a property. But news like that moved quicker in Cottageville than a dog after a dropped hotdog.

Sarah set her keys in the ceramic dish by the door, kicked off her boots, and put the muffin on the kitchen table. Whiskey sprawled on the rug like a tired sentinel, eyes half-lidded but ears alert.

Sitting on her sofa, she opened her laptop and typed "Paul Whitmore Iowa" into the search bar. The results were pitiful: a

LinkedIn profile with barely a job description, an old Facebook account that hadn't been updated in years, and one brief mention in a real estate transfer record from twenty years ago in Pennsylvania. No photos, no family tags, no "friends" who commented on birthdays or holidays.

"He was like a ghost," Sarah murmured, clicking from one dead-end link to another.

Whiskey shifted, his paw twitching in his sleep as though he were chasing something.

"Yeah, boy," Sarah said softly. "Feels like I'm chasing shadows, too."

Her phone buzzed. A text from Emily lit up the screen: "Did you hear the rumor? Someone says Paul worked for the government before he moved here. Secret job. Classified stuff."

Sarah's pulse quickened. She typed back: "Where did you hear that?"

"From Travis, of course," came the reply. "He says he overheard it at the salon. You know what that means..."

Travis, Emily's boyfriend, worked at Sergio's, the only salon in town that charged big city prices for their cuts, colors, and blow-outs. And it, like Java and Juice, contained more gossip than a tabloid magazine. Sarah smiled faintly before texting, "It means half the town will believe Paul was a CIA agent before dinner." Still, she couldn't shake the possibility. Quiet men with no pasts usually *had* one—it was just buried deeper than most.

She set the phone down and reached for the muffin. If she was going to be excavating dirt, she needed energy.

Because whatever Paul had been looking for, it hadn't stayed buried. Someone else knew, too. And someone had killed to keep it hidden.

CHAPTER 4

Saturday early afternoon sunlight slanted through the curtains of Sarah Carter's living room, painting little diamond shapes across the hardwood floor. Whiskey sprawled in the middle of them, belly up, tongue hanging out the side of his black gums, and snoring like a clogged trumpet being played by a drunk musician.

Sarah nudged his ear with her toe. "Don't get too comfortable, partner. We've got work to do."

The red heeler let out a deep huff and flopped dramatically onto his side in protest.

Sarah picked up her phone, scrolled through her contacts, and tapped the number for Lottie Brighton.

It rang four times, and Sarah was sure it would switch to voice mail when Lottie asked, "Is it really you, Sarah? You're calling instead of texting. Did someone die?" she joked. Ever since Lottie returned to L.A. they texted every couple of days, even when Sarah was with Jared in Prague.

"Uh..."

Whiskey had opened one eye like he was eavesdropping on Sarah's stumbling over speech.

"What's wrong?" Lottie pressed.

"Have the police called you?" Sarah didn't wait for an answer. "Whiskey and I found Paul Whitmore dead yesterday. He was dressed as a scarecrow and someone made him a part of the Halloween decorations in the park."

"Oh my God. That's crazy. Sounds like a scene from a slasher movie."

"I know. And of course, this town is buzzing with questions."

Lottie's voice was soft as she said, "As is your mind, I'm sure, Sarah."

"Well, I am curious who killed him. And why. Which is why I'm calling. Did he tell you how he heard you had a house to rent? Do you know where he's from or what his occupation is or why he came to Cottageville?" Sarah hated that she sounded like she had verbal diarrhea.

"I hired Katie Smith to manage the rental. She did the background check, credit score, and wrote the contract. All I know is she said his credit score was around 800 and that he seemed to have plenty of money to pay the rent. You'd have to ask her for more details."

Katie Smith had two Samoyeds, Babs and Tabs, which Sarah and Emily groomed monthly, and Katie was one of only two real estate agents Sarah knew of in town. It made sense that Lottie would hire someone local to manage her late father's house. "Okay. I'll phone Katie when we hang up. How was your trip?"

Lottie had spent the previous weekend on Oahu's North Shore with a pro surfer she had recently started dating. She filled Sarah in on all of the details of the trip, the awesome hotel villa they stayed in, the sea turtles she saw nesting on the beach, horseback riding, the spa, and...the alone time as the dude had spent more time on his board in the water than with her. "That made it a bust for me. I mean I was thrilled to be at Turtle Bay, but the relationship potential is dead in the water, pun intended." Her laugh was crisp like the click of boots on a marble floor.

"Nice one," Sarah said. "And that's too bad. At least you got a stellar vacay out of it."

"That's true. But it may have been better to go somewhere that wasn't known for world-class surfing."

"Hindsight."

"Hey, it's good to hear your voice, but I've gotta go. Thanks for calling. Text soon." Lottie disconnected.

Sarah's eyes logged movement outside. Janice Jenkins, who lived across the street, was raking leaves in her front yard. She wore an old pale pink sweater that appeared to be cashmere and army green chinos and tan deerskin gardening gloves. Though she was approaching her eighth decade, she was spry and a formidable force, doing top-secret work for governments for much of her life. If anyone would know if Paul Whitmore was CIA, it was Mrs. Jenkins. Sarah shoved her phone into her back pocket and told Whiskey to come. As she walked across the street, Mrs. Jenkins stopped raking and said, "Hello, Sarah. Whiskey, how's my favorite plant inspector." Her laugh sounded like paper being wrinkled.

Whiskey wagged as though he appreciated the title.

"Good afternoon," Sarah said, standing where Janice's yard and the street met. "Mind if I ask you something?"

"Is this about Paul?"

Sarah nodded. "Had you met him?"

"At the library a few times." Janice's blue eyes watered behind her glasses.

Sarah wondered if it was allergies.

She knew that Janice gave Daphne private French lessons in one of the library's meeting rooms on a weekly basis. Daphne had invited her to join them, but Sarah didn't have the time or the interest to improve her high school level French. "I heard he was looking for something in the old newspapers."

"Yes. Photos and I believe some kind of legal notice. He wasn't specific with me."

"Do you know in what time frame?"

"He didn't say and I didn't ask. But now that he has died, I'm assuming you and the police are trying to find a motive." Despite the teary-ness, Janice's eyes sparkled. She took off one glove and used her finger to wipe under her eye. "I had no idea when I moved here that the bur oak would do this to me. Raking kicks up the pollen."

"You could stop and let me and Jared handle it for you."

"Oh, that's okay, dear. It's one way for me to get exercise, though I should have taken an antihistamine before I started."

"One of the rumors spread around Cottageville is that Paul was CIA." Sarah paused and eyed her neighbor. Whiskey sat at attention near Sarah's left leg.

"People love to speculate. Did you know the odds of someone being a CIA agent is something like point oh one percent? You'd have been odds on some games in Vegas."

"Do you know his occupation?"

Mrs. Jenkins shook her head side to side and wiped her eye again with her bare hand. "He certainly didn't strike me as the dark glasses and trenchcoat type. Not that we really wear that. I guess he could have been an analyst or something for some government group. That's mainly research and quiet work...for people who like archives, old records, and computers." Janice pursed her lips together and frowned. "That's mind-numbing work."

"I see. Do you know if he had family?"

"I really don't know much beyond he spent time in the library looking at the paper. Oh, and he mentioned something about living in Syracuse at some point in his life. But I don't remember how that came up."

"Syracuse? As in Syracuse, New York?"

Mrs. Jenkins smiled. "The one in Sicily is spelled the same by Americans, but is actually Siracusa." Janice's Italian accent sounded perfect to Sarah's untrained ears. She knew her neighbor was fluent in a number of languages.

"I guess I'll head to the library next to see if Carole can provide more insight into Paul's research. Thank you for your time."

"You're welcome, Sarah. Any time. One thing I've wondered is if Paul dressed himself as a scarecrow to participate in the festivities or if the killer put him in costume. If it was the latter, what statement was the killer trying to make? Something to think about." Her voice trailed off.

"It most certainly is," Sarah said. "Thank you. Come on, Whiskey, let's walk back into town."

They walked up the hill and back through the park and then crossed over Main Street and walked a block north of Java and Juice. Cottageville Library had one wall of glass and steel that had been replaced earlier in the year after a big rig driver lost control and smashed into the building. Jared had been atop a ladder painting a holiday scene on the windows and somehow survived the impact. Sarah thought of that again as she approached the entrance and a chill ran through her of what she could have lost that day. She took a deep, cleansing breath, and opened the door for Whiskey and followed him inside. Upon seeing them, Carole Binds' expression brightened and a smile unfurled across her face, bunching her cheeks under her purple eyeglasses.

"Whiskey. Sarah. How are you both?" Her voice shattered the silence of the space.

Whiskey walked around the raised, circular desk so he had access to Carole, who bent to scratch his head.

Sarah glanced around and didn't see any patrons, so aloud she said, "Hi, Carole. We are well. Quiet day around here?"

Carole ran a hand through her flaxen wavy bob. "I've helped

people find books here and there and story hour was this morning. But there's not been a ton of traffic...this isn't exactly gossip central." She tittered and covered her mouth with her fingers.

"Sergio's and Java and Juice have that handled. Hey, I was told that Paul Whitmore spent a lot of time here looking through newspaper archives. Do you know what he was looking for?"

"Are you investigating, again, Sarah?" Carole's mouth corners tilted upwards.

"Eh. Chief James told me I could look into Paul's life, like figure out where he was from, what he did, what he was looking for. But he kinda forbade me to look into his death."

Carole's face broke into a grin and her eyes sparkled. "And is that your plan?"

Sarah returned the smile. "For now. I mean, no one seems to know much about Paul. At least no one I've talked to so far and my internet search results were sparse. Did you talk to him a lot? Did he tell you things?"

"He did spend time here. Many, many hours, in fact. And yes, he read a lot of the old newspapers. He also spent time paging through the local history books in the section over there." Carole's arm went straight out from her side and her finger was pointed to a shelving unit that was perpendicular to her desk.

"Do you know what he was looking for?"

"He spent a lot of time looking at legal notices and reading about the families who founded the town. He also photocopied a map of Cottageville he found in one of the old books and I saw him write some names and numbers on it. He never said what he was doing when he did that."

"Do you mean like he wrote the names of the town founders and the dates or was he creating a kind of plat map with the owners' names on the sections? Did he draw boundary lines?" Sarah's brow creased as she tried to envision what Paul might have done to the map.

"Maybe like a plat map. I'm not sure. I didn't get a good look at it. You may want to check with the city planning office. Maybe he inquired about property records for a specific time frame."

"Do you know why he was looking at the legal notices and the town history? Did it seem like he was doing research for a job or was it personal?"

Carole admitted she never asked him what he did for a living. She had assumed he might be retired, since he was in the library during business hours and sometimes spent all day looking through the archives and books.

"Do you know if he was single or if he had a family?"

Carole shook her head and her hair bounced a bit. "I never asked. I'm not even sure how old he was. Could have been in his fifties or sixties. I did tell him Mayor Trish's father might be a good person for him to talk to since the McGowans have been here for generations."

"The same with Gladys' late husband's family, right? The Rossmillers?"

"Yes, the Rossmillers have been here since the early 1900s, if not before. So have the few families with sizable farms on the outskirts of town. Bunky Buffalo's great-grandparents, or maybe it was his grandparents, owned a farm one hundred times bigger than the acres he now has. Same with Bill's family, though they were further out."

"Could Paul have been looking for land owned by his relatives back in the day? Do you know of any Whitmores in our area or any in the town's history?"

"I don't. But that doesn't mean they weren't here." She scratched Whiskey's head between his ears again and the cattle dog lovingly looked up at Carole and smiled. "Or it could have been his mom's side of the family tree."

"Do you know which books he read?"

Carole clicked some keys and the computer screen to her right came to life. "Umm, looks like he has two books out on loan right now, an older book called *Iowa History Reader* and one on Iowa and the Civil War. I guess I'll have to talk to Chief James about getting those back." Carole pursed her lips. She hit an up arrow on her keyboard and seemed to page through Paul's whole borrowing history. Then she said, "Follow me," to Sarah and walked towards the open part of her desk, with Whiskey on her heels.

Sarah trailed Carole to the shelving unit the head librarian had pointed at early. Carole stopped and crouched in front of a lower shelf of books. "This whole row and the bottom one. He's been through most of these and a few on the shelf above, though those are more history of the midwest as opposed to being Iowa-specific."

"Wow. That's a lot of books. And since I have no idea what I'm looking for—"

Carole cut her off with a chuckle. "It's the proverbial needle in a haystack or as I like to say, like finding that right lid for the mason jar in the back of the pantry."

Sarah chuckled. "In our house it is the lids for the plastic containers or the second sock in the pair. Always elusive."

"Exactly."

"Do you want to check out a few of the more local books and read through those, and I'll start reading through others? Maybe between the two of us, we can figure out what Paul was looking for."

"And if he found it," Sarah added. She grabbed the first six books from the shelf. "I'll start with these and I appreciate your help. Of course, maybe the police will find his notes and those two books and share their findings with us. That could be useful." She smirked, before walking her small pile of books toward the circulation desk. Whiskey and Carole followed, and Carole carried the next four books from the shelf.

"I'm excited to help you sleuth, Sarah. After yesterday, I was wishing I had spent more time talking to Paul and getting to know him. He seemed like a nice man. I'm not sure why someone wanted him dead, but I doubt he deserved it."

Sarah's voice was barely above a whisper. "No one deserves to be murdered." And even though she had promised Chief James she'd only look into Paul's life, she really, really wanted to find his killer.

Sarah thanked Carole for her time and for her help looking in the books for clues. She promised to be back in touch early the following week. And then she and Whiskey retraced their steps across Main Street, through the park—where all of the Halloween decorations had been removed and some parents pushed younger kids on the swings while older children climbed the jungle gym. Sarah's heart warmed that the park was again filled with laughter and joy. She wanted it to stay that way.

Before she left the park, Sarah asked Paul's ghost—which she wasn't sure she believed in—to show her the way. 'Tis the season, she thought wryly.

CHAPTER 5

Sarah had a whole chicken with veggies roasting in the oven by the time Jared arrived home from Java and Juice. Her culinary skills were limited, but that was one meal she made that was consistently beyond edible. She was grateful Jared had mastered the kitchen, which afforded them to eat well. Before he had moved into her house, Sarah had eaten a lot of salads, pasta, and things that were easy and fast to prepare.

Whiskey, who was lying on a love seat, opened one eye to confirm it was Jared who walked into the room. He swished his tail in greeting.

Jared said, "Hi, boy," and then bent to greet Sarah, who sat on the nearby sofa, with a kiss atop her messy bun. "You wouldn't believe all the tall tales that mingled with the scent of Ginger's pumpkin bars all day long."

"Tall tales as in you are sure they aren't true?" Sarah set aside the library book she was reading and the legal pad on which she was making notes.

Jared eyed the title. "Are you interested in Cottageville history now or is this tied to Paul Whitmore's death?"

"More like his life," Sarah said. "He was researching the town and its forefathers, Carole thinks."

"Does she know why?"

"No. But back to those 'tall tales' as you called them. Once, when Bill mentioned the town 'chewing on speculative stories', he compared gossip to a tough piece of meat and said it was 'hard to tell the gristle from the good stuff'."

"Colorful." Jared nodded his head. "And probably true in this case. Besides the rumors of witness protection and Paul being a spook, I heard that Paul was a private investigator working a case, had moved here so the family and wife he abandoned couldn't find him, and that he was running from the mob. Oh and my favorite over-the-top story of the day, that he was in town looking for fresh faces for porn."

"Holy cow. That's crazy. All of it. Why are people so quick to fill in the blanks with made-up nonsense?"

Jared rubbed her arm. "They are probably bored, and maybe subconsciously think everyone else's lives are much more exciting than theirs."

"Haven't the crimes around Cottageville made their lives exciting enough? I, for one, could use a little less of that kind of excitement." Sarah huffed.

Jared elbowed her playfully. "Umm, Miss Marple, I'm not sure I believe you. You thrive on solving mysteries and putting puzzles together."

Sarah avoided Jared's gaze as if she were a puppy who had chewed a new pair of boots. Silence dragged on before she mumbled, "Maybe..."

"So, how can I help you investigate?"

Sarah told Jared about her promise to Chief James, to only look into Paul's life.

"Where have you looked so far?"

"The internet. I couldn't find much. Maybe you can double check and see if you come up with anything different. And I talked to Bill, Janice, and Carole. Chief James said they don't yet know the cause of death. Or they didn't this morning. I told him I thought Paul had been killed elsewhere."

"Maybe, but that's not focusing on Paul's life," Jared teased. "I'm going to take a quick shower to wash off the cafe's pumpkin spice fall smells that have seeped into my pores. I have time before we eat, right?"

"If you are as quick as a drive-through carwash."

"That's quick, but I'll try. Then after we eat, I'll work with you to see if we can find out who Paul was and what he did and what he was doing in our town."

"Sounds good." Sarah smiled at him before she stood and walked into the kitchen to check on the chicken. Whiskey padded after her, either following his nose or more likely deciding it was time for his supper.

Ten minutes later, Whiskey had inhaled his food faster than a toddler with a piece of birthday cake, and Sarah and Jared were across from each other at the dining room table. Just as she was about to put a bite of chicken into her mouth, Sarah said, "Oh I forgot. You got a package." She pushed back from the table and scurried into the kitchen. She returned carrying a rectangular cardboard box about four inches in height. "From your publisher."

Jared's first graphic novel had been published in the spring and his second had been turned in to his publisher last month. He took the box from her and used his butter knife to poke into the tape and slice it open. When he opened the flaps, his cheeks bunched into a grin and his eyes filled with joy. "So cool." He pulled out four books, fanned them, and held them up to Sarah.

She looked at the covers, and said, "Japanese. Korean. Is that one Thai? And what's the last one?"

Jared chuckled. "Yes, Thai and Turkish."

"Wow. You've gone so global. Languages on every continent. I'm so proud of you."

"Not every, as it hasn't been translated into penguin." Jared's grin grew wider at his own joke.

Sarah said, "I'm not sure penguins can read," as he put the books back into the box and pushed it down the table a bit.

"Cute." Jared stabbed a carrot and put it in his mouth. After he swallowed, he said, "I really am living the dream. I'm grateful for all of the translations and the interest in the book. It's wild receiving email and DMs from fans. Some fangirl in Korea, who doesn't look more than sixteen in her profile pic, asked me on TikTok to marry her."

"Wait, what? Does she want to fight me?" Sarah chuckled. "I hope you let her down easy and told her you are spoken for?"

"Nope, I told her I'd only consider it if her dad threw in a solid dowry package–Rolex, Ferrari, and a house in the Caymans."

Stopping mid bite, Sarah glared playfully at Jared.

Responding to Sarah's 'that's not funny demeanor,' Jared said, "I'm kidding! So far I've ignored it." Changing the subject, he said, "Sarah, this chicken is really good. Did you add rosemary this time?"

"I did. Thank you for noticing. I can't believe someone suggested Paul Whitmore was a talent scout for porn. They might as well have suggested he was a headless horseman or a former President of the United States."

"Well, we'd all know that wasn't true. People know the names of the presidents."

"Not all of them. I bet most Americans couldn't name Tyler, Fillmore, and Chester Arthur."

"Okay. I'll give that. Rutherford Hayes I'd add to that list, too."

Sarah took a sip of water before saying, "I have no idea who that is."

"That's the point," Jared joked. "Anything you want to do tomorrow since we both have the day off?"

"I'd love to see if Katie Smith would let us into Paul's house."

"Yeah, I'm sure Chief James would be thrilled with that."

"But looking at a person's residence is a great way to get to know their life. Look at what we learned about Micas Brighton as we helped Lottie clean out her dad's estate."

"True. But it could be a crime scene."

"Can we at least drive by and see if the police have it cordoned off or are working there?"

He reached his left hand across the table and covered her left one, the one not holding her fork. "Yes, we can do that. Though you should know, Sarah, I'm only agreeing because I know if I don't, you'll go there yourself. Probably by yourself. And we don't know if that's safe."

Sarah smiled. "Thank you. And yep. That's totally what I would have done. But not alone. I'd take Whiskey." Her smile turned into a grin with the last three words.

"And he's been great in the line of fire, but I don't want either of you to go through that again. We will drive by tomorrow, nothing more. And then after, is there anything else you'd like to do? We haven't seen a movie in a while."

"Umm, I'm not sure I can concentrate on a movie when we have a mystery to solve." Sarah smirked and shrugged.

"Well, let's see how much we can uncover tonight." Jared finished the last few bites of vegetables left on his plate. "Thanks for dinner. It was delicious."

"You're welcome. I'm going to call Katie as soon as I load the dishwasher. Maybe she'll tell me previous addresses or anything else Paul put on his rental application."

"I'll help with the clean up." Jared picked up his plate and utensils and hers and carried them into the kitchen. Sarah followed with the leftover food.

When Whiskey heard the dishes being loaded into the dishwasher, he came in to investigate and to try to lick each dish as they slid them into the machine. "If you lick them clean," Jared said, "then we don't have to wash them. I can just put them back into the cupboard."

"Ew," Sarah said.

Laughter rumbled from Jared's chest as Whiskey's license tag got stuck on the dishwasher. "Hang on, boy. I'll get you free. Otherwise the whole drawer will go flying." He bent at the waist to unhook the ring holding the metal disk to Whiskey's collar that had looped onto the bottom rack's tine.

Whiskey backed away from the dishwasher with a low groan, like it was now his enemy.

"Silly dog," Sarah said, ruffling the fur between his ears.

He huffed once and then left the kitchen for the living room couch. Sarah followed after him, carrying her phone. She pulled up the contact information for Katie as she walked.

The phone rang once, twice, three times, and then on the fourth, it switched to voice mail. "Hey, Katie. It's Sarah. Lottie said you handled the rental of her dad's house to Paul Whitmore. I was wondering if you knew where he moved from. Can you call me back and let me know? Thank you."

Jared came into the living room and plopped onto the couch. He opened his laptop and started typing. Sarah sat next to him and picked up the library book she had been reading when Jared had come home and her notebook. She wasn't sure what she was looking for, but she hoped some kind of Spidey sense would kick in when she came across it—though she knew that might be a longshot. She only knew what books he had read, not what he was looking for.

But then something occurred to her.

"Hey, Jared, have you heard of any other Whitmores in town?"

"No. You?"

"No. Can you go to one of those online phone and address directories and look for the surname Whitmore in Cottageville and maybe surrounding areas?"

"Yeah, hang on a sec."

Sarah watched his screen as he opened another browser and did the search.

"None in Cottageville." He changed the city to "Cedar Rapids."

"Seventy-eight with the last name Whitmore. Oh, but they aren't all in Cedar Rapids. Looks like that's statewide."

"Let's look at all of them. See if there's a listing for Paul or a listing for anyone that has Paul listed as a family member."

The first name was Angela and it said she was in her twenties. No relative named Paul. Bartholomew was next, aged forty and a software developer. Five of his relatives were listed but not one of them was named Paul. On and on the alphabetical list went. At the P's, Paul's name was notably absent.

Sarah pursed her lips. "Why isn't he there?"

"Maybe he hasn't lived here long enough. When did he move in? One month ago? Two? Three at the most. I'm not sure where this data comes from or how often it gets updated, but it is possible there wasn't enough of a record of him being here."

"Could be. Can you ask Google where this website gets its information?"

"Sure." Jared opened another window and prompted that search. "Government records, property records, and other diverse sources," he read aloud.

"So he didn't own property here and wasn't here long enough to file a tax return. Maybe he didn't even go to the DMV. I know legally you're supposed to change your plates and license within thirty days, but I'll admit I wasn't quite that quick when I moved from Seattle." She lifted her eyes halfway from the screen and her lips tugged into a crooked half-smile as her cheeks flushed a light pink.

"I think I waited until exactly day thirty. That's one of the hassles of moving."

"Do you know what kind of car Paul drove?"

"Nope."

"Hmm. I guess we may see it if we drive by his place tomorrow. Maybe it's still in the driveway."

"Could be. Want me to finish going through this Whitmore list?"

"Yes, please."

"Are you going to read along with me?" Jared teased.

"No, sir. I'm going back to this book." Sarah picked up the book from her lap. She flipped to the index in the back to see what subjects were listed. The Buffalo surname jumped out at her toward the beginning of the list. Sarah scanned the list to see other last names she recognized: Larkins, Reid, McGowan. Other names she didn't recognize as belonging to her fellow townsfolk, but were common in the U.S., like Miller, Smith, and Brown. Sarah turned back to the page she had been reading when Jared had come home. A few minutes later, she said, "Did you know Cedar Rapids was founded in 1849 but that it was called Columbus?"

"No. No idea. Was Cottageville founded before or after that?"

"It was a few farms without any government structure. One of the farmers built a one-room schoolhouse for his kids and the neighbor kids and hired, what sounds to me, like the first teacher in these parts. Built a church, too. Methodist. Seems like from that structure and others moving to the area, that's how we eventually became a town. The farmer who started those things, his name was Thomas Smith. He's mentioned as the founding father of Cottageville."

"In what year?"

"1856. It's on the sign when you drive in on the main road. Under 'Welcome to Cottageville' it says '1856' in small type."

"Huh. I've seen the sign but never paid attention to the date. Must have looked completely different back then."

"Most definitely. Big farms. Lots of corn and cattle. Dirt roads, I'm guessing, for the horses and maybe horse-drawn carriages."

"Any old photos in that book?"

Sarah paged through quickly searching for black and white images. "Not in this one, but probably in one of the others." She grabbed another book off the coffee table and fanned through it, stopping when she came to a small brick building with the word bank engraved over the door. Sarah frowned, reading the caption. "This says First Cottageville Bank, built in 1900. I wonder where this is and what happened to it. Have you ever seen it?" She shoved the book toward Jared.

"No, it doesn't exist any more. And all of the banks in town are part of Bank Iowa or a national brand."

Sarah frowned. "Just like so many businesses. They start small and then get consumed by or driven under by the big guys. There should be room for all of us."

Jared put his arm around her and pulled her to him. "I agree. Though I also understand how people don't want to spend a lot so the smaller businesses can't compete on pricing when the big guys get volume discounts."

"I'm glad there's no groomers or pet chain places within forty or fifty miles. Otherwise..." Sarah's voice trailed off.

"Your customers are also loyal. They love you and Em, and it is clear to everyone how much you love their pets."

"True. Except for maybe Chutney," Sarah admitted. Chutney was a Chihuahua who acted like a Tasmanian devil. He lived with George, who owned Produce and More, and his wife, both in their late sixties. Sarah wasn't sure how they put up with the snarly little beast who bit any chance he got. Sarah had bought long leather gloves for Emily and herself for any time they had to cut Chutney's nails or bathe him. It was the only way to keep their arms and hands safe. It was amazing how much damage a five-pound terror could cause in a couple of seconds.

"I'm sure if George was honest, he'd admit to not liking Chutney sometimes, too."

"Anyway, back to Paul Whitmore. You scour the internet and I'll keep looking in these books." Sarah flipped through looking at more photos. Where the bank was in the 1900s could have been on Main Street. It was difficult to tell. Sarah turned the page and an image made her audibly suck in a breath.

"Find something good?" Jared asked.

"Yes, look at this." She shoved the book onto his laptop keyboard. The photo was of a two-story Victorian with a big porch right along the dirt road. "Look familiar?"

"It looks like Maslow's Antique Store."

"I think it is." Sarah looked for a number on the building but there wasn't one. Then again, she thought, in the early 1900s none of the buildings were probably numbered. Addresses weren't so specific then, especially in rural areas.

Sarah squinted at a faded, handwritten script below the photo. She could make out a W and what she thought was an h and maybe a t in the first word along with a capital H and squiggles that could have been an o-u-s-e. "Does that first word look like Whitmore to you?"

"Maybe. Or could be Whitman or White something. It's pretty faded and illegible." Sarah flipped to the cover of the book. "The author's name is Samuel Smith. Can you Google him? Does he live in Cottageville? I've never heard of him. I wonder where he got the photos for the book."

Jared typed "Samuel Smith Cottageville" into the search engine, but was interrupted from looking into the results when they heard the ambulance with its siren screeching and coming down their street—which had only six houses so they knew it had been called for someone they knew.

Sarah flew off the sofa and ran to the door with Whiskey at her heels and Jared bringing up the rear.

Wendy and Walter Parks exited both sides of their rig and ran to Mrs. Jenkins' front door. They tried to open it and found it locked.

Sarah grabbed a key from a bowl on the console table by the front door and raced across the street in her socks. She yelled as she ran, "I have a key."

CHAPTER 6

endy and Walter each carried a medic bag. They stood back and allowed Sarah to unlock the door. "Janice, Janice," Wendy called as they entered.

Janice Jenkins wore a flannel nightgown that reached to her shins. She was slumped in a wingback chair with her head at an angle.

"Oh my God!" Sarah exclaimed. She wanted to help her neighbor but knew she needed to hang back and let the professionals attend to the situation.

"Pulse is weak but steady," Wendy said to Walter.

"Heartbeat is strong," Walter replied.

Wendy jostled Mrs. Jenkins slightly. "Janice. Can you hear me? Janice, can you wake up?"

"She fainted?" Sarah asked, before she realized the words were coming out of her mouth.

Jared stood in the doorway behind her with Whiskey on his leash. "Sarah, I brought you some shoes," he said, barely above a whisper.

She turned to him and reached for her fleece-lined boots. "Thank you."

Walter hooked Janice up to a portable machine to monitor her vitals. Wendy talked to her, asking her to open her eyes. Tension snapped in the air around them for seconds that felt much longer to Sarah.

Finally, Janice opened her eyes. She looked disoriented and her eyes were unfocused.

"Janice. It's Walter and Wendy Parks. You called nine-one-one and said you were dizzy and needed help."

"I'll go get the chair," Walter said and he moved to leave the living room.

"Sarah, take Whiskey. I'll help Walter carry the chair up the stairs." Jared handed the leash to the love of his life before meeting Walter at the back of the ambulance.

"Do you remember anything?" Wendy asked Janice.

"I remember calling and then needing to sit down. I didn't want to fall. That's it."

To Sarah, Janice's eyes appeared clearer.

Wendy shined a penlight in the left eye and then the right,

talking Janice through what she was doing. "We're going to take you to the hospital for some tests. Your blood pressure is low, too low, in fact. Is it usually low?"

"It's low-ish as opposed to high, but I've never fainted before."

"Are you on any medications?"

"No."

"None at all?"

"Not a one. I know it's rare in today's day and age when doctors give pills for everything."

"Yes, It is rare. When's the last time you ate and what did you have?"

"I ate tuna salad on toast for supper with a cup of peppermint tea. No caffeine."

"Did you make the tuna salad?"

"Yes. It was fresh from the can. Albacore."

Walter pushed the chair into the room. He and Wendy each grabbed one of Janice's biceps and helped her pivot from the wingback chair to the gurney chair. But as she rose to just about standing, she fainted again so they transferred her while she was unconscious and strapped her in.

"Blood pressure is coming back up," Wendy said. "Janice, honey, open your eyes. Look at me."

Whiskey strained at his leash like he wanted to go to his neighbor and help.

Half a minute passed and finally Janice opened her eyes again. She glanced around the room like she wasn't sure where she was.

"We're taking you to the hospital," Walter explained, squatting in front of her so they were eye to eye. "Sarah will lock up your house. She is right behind you, along with Jared and Whiskey."

"It's okay, Mrs. Jenkins," Sarah said, walking around to the front of the chair. "Do you want me to call Bill and Gladys?" Bill and Gladys were her closest friends—or maybe more if those Cottageville rumors were to be believed—and Bill also had her power of attorney, as Sarah had learned earlier in the year when Bill had a heart attack while at a concert in the park.

For the first time in the seven years that Sarah had known her, Sarah thought Mrs. Jenkins looked frail. And that broke her heart. The octogenarian always seemed as robust as people half her age.

"Yes, Sarah. But tell them not to visit tonight. I'm very tired." Janice closed her eyes as Walter, Wendy, and Jared tilted the ambulance chair backwards a bit and then carried it down the stairs. Wendy and Walter slid it onto the tracks inside the ambulance and locked it into place with Wendy crawling in after it.

"Thank you for your help," she said before shutting the back doors.

Sarah rubbed her hands over her arms like she was chilled. After the ambulance pulled away and started up the street, she unclipped Whiskey from his leash and said, "Let's go home." Then she locked Janice's front door and followed Whiskey and Jared across the street.

When she got inside, she grabbed her phone off of the living room coffee table and noticed she had missed a call from Katie Smith. She didn't even check the message before she initiated a three-way call with Bill and Gladys. "Hey, Janice apparently called nine-one-one because she was feeling faint. The Parks just took her to the hospital.

Her blood pressure is too low. She asked me to call you both but said not to visit tonight as she's too tired."

"Like we'd leave her to go through this alone," Gladys said. Gladys was a retired art teacher and lived with two miniature poodles named Kahlo and Cassatt. Gladys was also Sarah's adopted grandmother as she had been Gigi's best friend.

"I'll pick you up in five minutes, Glad," Bill said.

"Do you need us to take the dogs?" Sarah asked.

"No, dear. I think they will be fine by themselves for a few hours. But if we end up staying longer than that, I'll call you. Thank you."

"And thank you for calling us, Sarah," Bill said.

"You're welcome."

Sarah disconnected and then listened to Katie's message. She told Sarah that she had run a credit and background check on Paul Whitmore and she checked three references. "He said he was retired, but didn't say from what. I didn't ask for a previous address, but I'm sure it is on the credit report," the message said. "I'll be in the office on Monday and can look for you then."

Sarah relayed the information to Jared. "Sort of progress," she said.

'Hey, hon, I'm not feeling much in a sleuthing mood right now, after Janice and everything. I hope she's going to be okay. Can we make some hot cider and watch something funny on streaming and then go to bed?"

Sarah wrapped her arms around him. "Of course. You worked today and were up before dawn's crack. I'm sure you're tired. I'll go heat the cider, and you find what you want us to watch." She gave him a peck on the lips and went into the kitchen.

She put a cinnamon stick into the pot and dumped in a couple of cups of apple cider from Produce and More. Once it was steaming, she poured the golden liquid into two mugs and carried them to the sofa. Whiskey was curled against Jared and the television was set to start a half-hour sitcom that they had seen many times before but that still made them laugh like children.

By the time the show ended, their cider was gone, and Whiskey stood at the back door waiting to be let out for his "last call."

"Any word on Janice?" Jared asked as he headed towards the bedroom and Sarah went to assist her red heeler.

Sarah checked her phone. Gladys had texted that the doctors had done bloodwork and were planning a scan of Janice's head to rule some things out. She was alert and fine as long as she stayed seated or lying down.

When Sarah and Whiskey entered the bedroom, she relayed the information from Gladys. Jared asked, "So vertical is the problem?"

"Sounds like it."

"I hope they figure out the cause and that it is an easy fix."

"Does she need us to go get the dogs or for one of us to go stay with them?" Jared walked into the bathroom and Sarah heard his electric toothbrush start.

She texted the question to Gladys.

When he came out of the bathroom, Sarah said, "Gladys said Janice told them to go home. She said she's stable and they need sleep."

Jared chuckled. "Sounds like her. Rational and quietly

authoritarian."

"Don't forget regal. She's often dressed like the Queen of England or the Queen Mum."

"True. And she's a survivor. She will get through this, I'm sure."

"I sure hope you are right," Sarah said. She turned off the nightstand liamp and emulated a big spoon around her man.

Long before the sun streamed through the bedroom window, Sarah awoke to her cattle dog standing on her chest, his cold, wet nose pressed against the tip of hers. "Get off, dog. What time is it?" she mumbled, reaching for her phone on the nightstand. Not quite five a.m.

"Can't we sleep a little while longer?" she asked Whiskey.

He gave a little whine and pushed off of her before bouncing to the floor. He ran to the bedroom door and gave one yip, commanding her to follow.

That's when she realized the other half of the bed was empty. Her eyes looked toward the bathroom, where she was greeted by the open door. "Okay, boy. I'm coming."

She padded after the dog in her flannel pj pants, patterned with a navy background with white bones scattered all over them. Her navy tank top was emblazoned with a red heeler head inside a heart.

At the back door, she let Whiskey out, and then followed her nose after the enticing aroma of freshly brewed coffee. She poured herself a cup, let Whiskey back into the house and fed him some grain-free kibble, and then walked down the hall to find Jared in his studio.

"Couldn't sleep?" she asked, before eying his empty coffee mug. "Want a refill?"

"Good morning, love." He pulled her into an embrace. "Too used to the early mornings at the cafe so I figured I'd use the time to get some work done." His adjustable reclaimed wood table had been a gift from Sarah when he first moved in. It was covered with drawings, some outlined in black ink and some shaded in—the third book in his series, though it wasn't under contract yet with the publisher. Jared's original deal was for two books with an option of first right-of-refusal on any future graphic novels. His first book had done so well that they had moved up the release date for book two to next spring. Sarah— and his agent—was sure that the publisher would sign him for many more books—and the agent thought maybe they could get a bid war going if he was willing to publish with competitors. Jared told Sarah he felt loyalty to the editor and publisher who had given him his start. But they had yet to make him an offer.

Jared had confidence that they would, so he was working on book three and had been outlining books four and five in the series. He now had enough fans all over the world that the books would sell, whether he published with a big house or self-published.

Sarah picked up his coffee mug and took it into the kitchen for a refill. When she returned to Jared's studio, she asked, "Did you want to keep working or walk with us this morning?"

"When are you going?"

"Maybe thirty minutes."

"Yeah, I'll go. But I'll wait to shower until we get back."

"Okay. That's where I'm headed now. It looks like the leaves outside may be a bit crunchy, like the temperature dropped close to freezing last night." Sarah and Jared both looked out his big window. Blades of grass looked like frosted soldiers in the back deck lighting.

When Sarah walked through the bedroom, cradling her coffee cup, she found Whiskey in the middle of their bed lying on his back with all four paws in the air and his head lolled to the side. "Silly dog," she muttered on her way into the bathroom. She took a healthy slug of her black beverage before starting the shower.

Forty minutes later Jared came into the backyard where Whiskey was having a staring competition with Mozart...or rather he had the cat in his chocolate eyed crosshairs and the cat sat atop the fence side-eying the dog while licking the length of one leg and then another. "Come on, dog," Sarah urged.

"I wondered what was keeping you," Jared said. "I should have known."

"He's been out here for almost ten minutes. No amount of verbal conjoling or coaxing or offering of chicken chews has moved him."

Jared walked to Whiskey and stuck his finger in the dog's collar and gave a single tug. "Come on, boy. We're going for a walk. I'll race you to the front door."

Whiskey turned his head at an angle and his eyes met Jared's, and then he was off like a greyhound after a rabbit. Jared laughed as he sprinted after the cattle dog. Sarah jogged after them, knowing they wouldn't leave without her. Over her shoulder she called, "Mozart, one of these days you're gonna press your luck. You know he can reach the top of the fence, right?"

Sarah wistfully looked at Janice Jenkins' house as they passed on their way up the hill. She said a silent prayer that her neighbor was well and would be home soon.

In the park, they took the path that weaved past the grandstand and evergreen that was ceremonially lit every December 1; passed by the children's playground with its jungle gym, merry-go-round, and swings, plus the sandpit for the little ones; neared the ball fields and the open spaces where people often ran their dogs; and then ended up where the Halloween booths had been and the entrance to the park from Main Street. Whiskey strode right from the stone exit to go to Bill's, but Sarah stopped to stare at what was hanging from the park entrance.

"Jared, look. Whiskey, hold up." She pointed her finger at what looked like a doll, hanging from a noose from the lampost that topped the short stone wall. Upon closer inspection, she realized it was clothed in a uniform with a small badge pinned to its chest and a name embroidered on the other side. It said "Order." The doll had short brown hair and wore a cop's cap.

"Holy crap," Jared said. "It's an effigy of Chief James. Tiny black cloth boots and all."

Sarah whipped out her phone and took a photo and then called the Chief, whose number was programmed to speed dial on her phone from all the previous Sherlock Holmes type adventures.

He answered on the second ring and sounded like she had woken him. "Sarah?"

"Um. You really need to come to the park. Someone made a doll of you and a noose and hung it from the light at the entrance on Main

Street."

"Like a voodoo doll?" He sounded annoyed as opposed to frightened.

"No pins in it. More like an effigy."

"How do you know it is me?"

"Says Order on the chest of the uniform."

"I'll be there in ten minutes. Stand guard and don't touch anything or let anyone else touch anything." Sarah was about to disconnect when she heard, "Hey, Sarah, are you alone?"

"No. Jared and Whiskey are with me."

"Good. Good. See you soon."

"Could be someone's idea of a sick joke," Jared said.

"Maybe. But after Paul's neck was broken by maybe a hanging, it's super creepy to find someone hanging a doll not far from where I found Paul and that it isn't random but made to look like a specific person."

Jared nodded his head yes just as a black and white car, lights off, pulled the curb. Candace Grimes, Cottageville's only female police officer and one of Sarah's friends, got out of the car. "You. Again," she joked to Sarah. "I should have known."

"Hey, I don't try to find mysteries. They just happen and I stumble upon them."

"More like you're magnetic north and they are all compasses."

"Wow. Complicated analogy." Sarah smirked.

"I try." Candace grinned. She turned her head one way and the other, looking at the doll tied to the lamp post, reminding Sarah of Whiskey when he was checking things out or listening intensely. "It's not a bad likeness for being made of cloth."

"Right. And someone went to a lot of trouble to make the belt and little boots and hat."

A luxury full-size SUV pulled up behind Candace's police car and Chief James, dressed in a gray sweatshirt and blue jeans, stepped down from the vehicle.

"New car?" Sarah asked.

"Barbara's brother is in town and he was blocking me in and still asleep so I grabbed his keys." Chief James shrugged.

"Nice ride."

"He's a banker. Wow. That does look a lot like me, in a flatter face kind of way." The eyes and mouth had been drawn onto the face with marker. The nose had a bit of stitching and fiber fill to erupt slightly from the facial plane.

Both Candace and Chief James took photos of the doll from all angles, and then wearing gloves, Chief James removed the doll from the black light fixture. They photographed the back side of it that wasn't visible from where it hung. And then it was enclosed in an evidence bag.

"Thanks for calling me, Sarah."

"Do you think it is a prank or something more nefarious?" But before he could answer, she asked, "Do you think it's related to Paul's death?"

"Don't know. Don't know. And don't know." Chief James grinned, which caused Candace and Jared to chuckle.

Sarah frowned and mumbled, "I hate it when there's so many things we don't know."

"Babe, that's part of life." Jared put his arm around Sarah and pulled her against his side. Then he kissed the top of her head.

The radio at Candace's shoulder crackled with information about a fender bender on the state route. She said her goodbyes, hopped in her car, and took off with the siren wailing. Chief James thanked Sarah one more time, before getting back into the borrowed SUV.

Sarah looked over at Bill's vacant porch. She figured he had been at the hospital until late. She said to Whiskey, "We'll come back and see Bill later today. Once he's awake."

And then they turned and walked back through the park the way they had come.

CHAPTER 7

Jared made them French toast with plenty of cinnamon and ginger and topped with fresh fruit for breakfast. Then, after the kitchen was cleaned, Sarah said she wanted to drive past Micas Brighton's house "just in case there was something to see."

"Okay," Jared said. "But we will not break and enter, nor am I going through any trash."

Flashes of her and Ginger climbing into a Dumpster to look for clues after a proprietor of a candy shop had been attacked last year flitted through Sarah's mind. That had been crazy and gross but also fun. The corners of her mouth tilted upward at the thought. "Okay. No going through trash. That's kind of my and G's thing anyway."

"Um, yeah. I don't want to horn in on that fun." Jared rolled his eyes like a teenage girl. "So besides doing the drive by, what else is on our agenda? Last night you said no to a movie. So bowling? Mini-golf? Hike? We haven't schlepped out to the water tower for a few months."

Sarah's life had been threatened last year in the woods between her house and the field where the water tower had stood for decades. She had little desire to go through that part of her neighborhood again, even though the police had arrested the perpetrator.

"Maybe we'll skip the water tower. Let's do the drive by now. Or..." Sarah glanced at the time. "I'll text Janice first and see how she is. Then we'll do the drive by and then come back home for more Paul Whitmore research. We can walk Whiskey after that and then go to maybe a three o'clock movie, which would get us back home in time for dinner. How's that sound?"

"Ok, so you changed your mind on the movie? Sweet, that works for me."

Sarah texted Janice and received a response almost immediately. "Electrolyte imbalance and too low of sodium. Head scan looked fine. Said I might be released this afternoon."

"Oh good," Sarah wrote back. "Do you need us to come and get you?"

"Glad and Bill will. Thank you. And thank you for letting the Parks in. So much better than them having to break a window or bust through the door. :)"

"You're welcome. We are here if you need anything."

Sarah set her phone on the kitchen counter and looked at Jared.

"Such a relief. Sounds like they are giving her an IV with some stuff to rebalance her body and they will send her home."

"Did she say how she got out of balance?"

"No, but I think it can happen if you drink too much water or not enough or if your body isn't absorbing nutrients. But I'm not a doctor nor do I play one on TV."

"Of course you aren't. But you are a smart cookie." He leaned over and kissed her.

"Chocked full of nuts, right?"

"A little bit nuts, but in a very good way." Jared's grin caused his green eyes to sparkle. "Now, come on, mi'lady, we have a house to scope out. Are we taking your trusty steed or mine? And I'm sure our jester sidekick will insist on coming along for the ride."

"Most definitely, fine sir." Sarah held her hands to her sides holding an imaginary skirt and curtsied in the silly schtick they had done since right after they met many years ago. "Since the CJ is blocking you in, we can take it."

Sarah grabbed Whiskey's leash just in case they ended up needing it. She shoved her feet without socks into her fleece-lined boots. The temperature high was going to be fifty-three today, but it was still chilly and a breeze had picked up in the last hour. Sarah was glad she had put a green merino wool sweater over her t-shirt.

The drive to the house owned by Lottie Brighton took eighteen minutes as the house sat on the edge of town without many close neighbors. From the street nothing marked the house as a possible crime scene. Sarah encouraged Jared to travel up the gravel driveway, praying they wouldn't get to the house and find it crawling with crime scene technicians. She didn't want to have to make excuses for their—really her—snooping.

No cars were in the unpaved driveway. Micas Brighton's two-story farmhouse was white with black shutters and three gables framing double windows. The roof was green metal and cement stairs led to the white front porch. The house seemed to be in good repair for its age, which Sarah estimated could be one hundred. But Sarah's thought upon seeing it again was the same as the first time she had ever laid eyes on it: the house was boring. It was a rectangle with three gables and what looked like a later addition to create the attached two-car garage. Its two doors lacked windows, so they couldn't see if Paul Whitmore's car was parked within.

Sarah knew from previous visits that the inside of the house was much more inspired, as Micas Brighton had an artist's eye. But today, police tape marked the front door and warned everyone not to enter. It reminded Sarah of Halloween scenes some of the Cottageville residents created in their yards. Tombstones, zombies, caution tape, and the works, celebrating a holiday of ghouls, goblins, the supernatural, and tricks and treats and childhood fun. Except this caution tape was not hung in good humor; it was as serious as a hanging.

As the CJ idled in front of the clearly vacant house, Sarah unclipped her seatbelt, opened the passenger door, and stepped down with Whiskey jumping over her seat to follow her.

"Where are you going?" Jared's eyes were narrowed and his brow furrowed. "I said we'd drive by. That's it."

"I just want to circle the house once to make sure no windows were broken or the side door isn't ajar or busted," Sarah said through the still open Jeep door.

"Sarah, please. I'm sure Chief James doesn't want you poking around here. It's still a crime scene."

"The quicker I can circle the house, the quicker we'll be gone. You can wait here if you want." Sarah shut the door. As she and Whiskey started around the right side of the house, she heard the engine stop and the driver's side of her vehicle creak open and then close. Jared's feet crunched on the gravel after them.

Sarah eyed the side door. The pane of glass was still in place. The wood was solid. She debated covering her hand with her sweater sleeve and checking if the door knob turned.

"Don't even think about it," Jared said, snaking an arm around her waist.

Sarah hated when he could read her mind.

Whiskey sniffed the ground and followed his nose on a trail invisible to them. He went right toward a tree and circled it, black nose wriggling at the scent. Then he took off at a jog diagonally across the backyard, nose to the grass.

"Raccoon. Possum. Maybe even a fox." Jared watched Whiskey as he simultaneously steered Sarah around the back right corner of the house.

Sarah eyed the trees at the edge of the backyard. She gauged if any had branches low enough to reach but high enough to hang a man. None had obviously been used for that purpose. And from what she could tell from the distance she was, the bases of the trees nor the ground around them showed any signs of disturbance. She turned her focus back to the house. No windows were cracked or broken. All were closed. The blinds were down and the curtains were pulled together. The back door was shut and its shade was drawn. Sarah wondered if the police had done those things or if Paul or his killer had left them that way.

She called to Whiskey, "Come on, boy. Follow us," as she walked with Jared to the far side of the house and back around to where they had parked. Whiskey gave up the trail and chased after them, jumping onto the passenger seat as soon as Sarah had opened the CJ's door. "Get in back, bud," she encouraged, sliding into the seat the dog had vacated.

When Jared got into the driver's seat, he asked, "Where to next?"

"I don't know. The walk-around was a bust. I had hoped to find a clue."

"Finding the effigy of Chief James wasn't enough for one day?" Jared playfully poked her in the ribs with his elbow.

"That was something. But I'm not sure it is related to Paul Whitmore's death."

Jared started the engine and then did a three-point turn so that they could drive down the long driveway, as opposed to backing down it.

"I just wish we knew more about him so we'd know where to look next. All I know is that he lived here, briefly, and frequented the library. That's not much to go on."

"It isn't, but you may have another lead tomorrow, when you talk to Katie. Maybe for today, we can focus on ourselves and have fun." Jared patted her leg. "What do you say? Want to go for a hike?

We could drive into the big city and go to the nature center. It's dog friendly."

Whiskey gave a woof from the backseat.

Jared chuckled. "The nature center has his vote."

"We can do that, if you don't mind the drive."

"It's only a half an hour. And while we do that, can you search on your phone for dog-friendly restaurants? I don't know if patios will be open this time of year, but I'd like to do the five-mile trail, and then grab lunch at the taproom or somewhere before we drive home."

"Sounds good." Sarah reached over and caressed one of Jared's fiery curls. "Thank you. You're right. I can't be on all of the time. Some fresh air and fall sunshine will be good for us."

On the drive to the nature center, Sarah couldn't shake an unease uncoiling in her low belly.

"You're quiet," Jared said.

"Just thinking."

"About Paul Whitmore?"

"About how he fit here—or didn't. He was a stranger who showed up, stayed for a blink, and now he's the center of a murder investigation. Doesn't that feel...off to you? Too quick?"

"Small towns notice newcomers. Maybe someone didn't like what they noticed."

She shot him a look. "Like who?"

He shrugged. "Could be anyone. Or maybe it's not about Cottageville at all—maybe trouble followed him."

Sarah turned her gaze out the window. She'd known every pothole and picket fence in this town, but Paul Whitmore had been a blank page. That blank page was now stained with blood.

Sarah's phone buzzed. It was a text from Janice that read, "Home now. Tired but okay. Thank you again."

Sarah smiled. "Good news. Janice is home."

"That is good news."

Just then Jared turned from the state route onto the paved entrance to the nature center. Whiskey sat up in the back seat, his nose to the air, sniffing. His body vibrated in excitement.

"Let's take the trail that goes around the lake," Sarah suggested as Jared pulled into the parking space.

He immediately killed the engine. "Okay, sounds good." Jared reached behind his seat to grab Whiskey's leash. "Stay by the car, Whisk. I'll need to hook you up."

Whiskey cocked his head so one of his ears was like a unicorn horn.

"Silly dog," Sarah mumbled, jumping down from the Jeep and taking a step back so as not to get hit by the cattle dog who was anxious to explore the new territory.

The path was dappled with sunlight and shadow from the nearby bur oaks and the silver maples, which had the most muted fall colors—the palest yellow Sarah had ever seen. "Look at those trees." She pointed toward the sky. "It's like a watercolor version of autumn, compared to the opulent oil color crimson of the sumac."

"You sound like the artist in our household," Jared joked. "Check out the purple on that dogwood. I've never seen it look like that. I've seen them yellow and red but not with all three colors."

"It's gorgeous."

Whiskey rustled through the cattails at the water's edge, startling a small wren who shot from the cluster of reeds like a pea from a shooter.

"Be careful, boy," Sarah said. "Don't slip in the mud and fall in."

Sarah twined her fingers with Jared's as she breathed in deeply the scent of earthy perfume and damp leaves. The water's mineral coolness lingered, mingling with the warm, nutty scent of fallen acorns crushed underfoot. It was the kind of fragrance that felt both nostalgic and alive, a quiet reminder that seasons, like life, brought constant change. "This has been a challenging year for our older friends," Sarah acknowledged. "First Bill's heart attack in June and now Janice's health emergency." She frowned. "I don't like the thought of not having them in our lives. I'm not ready for that."

Jared squeezed her hand. "Me neither. But they are healthy. Or at least they seem to be. Let's not focus on what might happen. Let's enjoy our time here and soak in the sunshine and this beautiful afternoon while we can." Jared stopped walking and pulled Sarah to him in a hug. "I love you, Sarah. I'm glad we can take a few hours and just be. You and me and the mutt." He grinned while looking into her eyes. Then he planted his lips against hers in a sweet kiss, before pulling her further down the path.

Whiskey trotted ahead, zigzagging from the path to the reeds and grasses along the water's edge and back again. He seemed to love all of the new smells and the adventure.

When they got halfway around the lake, they came across a tree stump and chainsawed sections of trunk. The stump itself had a big crack, like the oak tree had split, most likely across the path and into the water. The cut sections had been left on either side of the path. Sarah traced the growth rings with her finger before counting them. "It's older than me," she said, which meant it was also older than Jared since he was three years younger than Sarah.

Sarah marveled that some of the rings seemed to be double the thickness of others. She wondered what caused that. And one of the rings seemed to bump against another.

"Check this out," she said to Jared, pointing to the place where the two rings touched. She frowned as a thought occurred to her. "Hey, do you know that game six degrees of Kevin Bacon?"

"Yes."

"How many degrees of separation do you think there is between each person in Cottageville?"

"Two, maybe."

"I think we are all like these rings. Close together and part of the same whole. I mean, we've been talking about how much we don't know anything about Paul Whitmore, but maybe we are looking at it incorrectly. All of us, we are rings of the same town tree. We just haven't figured out who the closest ring is to Paul. Someone in town must have known him way better than we do. We need to find that person." Sarah's eyes sparkled as she talked aloud through the seed of a plan that was taking root.

"So you think trying to track down information about him is the wrong way to go? It's how we started the Micas Brighton case."

"It is and it worked well for that because learning about Micas Brighton was easy. He had a huge online footprint and a lot of professional credibility. But so far, we've unearthed little about Paul.

So I think—other than me talking to Katie tomorrow—that instead of focusing on Paul's life or death we should spend time asking the people we encounter every day if they knew him and were his friends. Who interacted with him and under what circumstances?" Sarah walked faster down the path, and Jared increased the length of his steps, stretching his long legs, to catch up with her. Whiskey raced past both of them to take the lead.

"Sarah, wait up, I'd like your hand again. Though I know the romance is lost now that you're concocting a mission." His dimple flickered into view, a fleeting spark of charm that softened the edge of his words, as if he hoped a hint of boyish mischief might keep her from slipping too far into detective mode.

She grabbed his hand and wrapped her fingers with his, but she wouldn't meet his eyes. "Sorry," she mumbled. "But do you like my idea?"

"I do. It's casting a much wider net."

"I'll need your and Ginger's help though, since Java and Juice is gossip central."

"It's one of them," Jared said, "but we aren't the only one. The texting and phone calls and whispers on front porches spread rumors faster than wildfires tearing through dry prairie grass, leaving no secrets unscorched."

"Well, aren't you the poet," Sarah teased, kissing the stubble on his left cheek.

"Hey, I could have not agreed to help." His green eyes sparkled and the right side of his mouth quirked upward as he added, "Or I could have been super cheesy and juvenile and told you I'd rather make like a tree and leave."

Sarah rolled her eyes. "Oh, brother. I'm so glad you didn't. I think that's the first time I've heard that since my elementary school days."

"Speaking of which," Jared said, as the path came to an end back at the parking lot where they left the CJ, "do you think there's any chance Paul Whitmore could have grown up here or spent summers here when he was a boy like you did?"

"I don't know." Sarah waited for Jared to unlock the door.

"I just keep thinking that there has to be a reason he moved to our town. We need to find that reason."

"We will, Jared. We will." Sarah's intuition assured her that they would. And she believed it.

CHAPTER 8

By seven-thirty the next morning, Sarah had already had one cup of coffee, walked Whiskey, visited with Bill, and grabbed breakfast, more coffee, and chipotle and lime chicken salads for lunch at Java and Juice before unlocking the Carter's Canine Coiffure for the day. The Coiffure, nestled on Rosewood Drive between an Italian restaurant and a dry cleaner, had once been a family's home. Sarah had remodeled it, combining several rooms so that the front door now opened into a cozy waiting room area with chairs, a sofa, and a large counter—its hinged section separating the space from the grooming area, which had once been the kitchen and dining room. The grooming area contained steel tables sporting poles alongside with leather loops to hold a dog's head, and stainless steel washing bins lined the wall, some at waist height and one at the ground level that was walk-in. Shelves of products and towels neatly stacked were anchored to the wall above the tubs.

The back rooms of the Coiffure consisted of a full bathroom, a breakroom, and a room stacked with dog crates that no one ever used. All dogs that came for grooming were well-behaved, except for Chutney, but a cage would do nothing to curb the chip on her shoulder, lashing-out behavior.

Sarah slid her denim dog-print apron over her head and double-wrapped it around her waist, just as the front door opened and Emily burst through. Her hair was dyed black and was in two braids like a goth Pippi Longstocking. She wore a pumpkin orange long sleeve t-shirt dress that hit two inches above her knees over ripped black tights and her Doc Marten boots. A black backpack weighted down her shoulder like it was filled with a fifty-pound boulder.

"Wow. Don't you look festive."

"'Tis the season and all that crap. You're early. I thought I'd come in while it was quiet and take my online quiz." Emily had finished an associate's degree and was now enrolled in a canine nutrition program.

"Don't let us stop you. We'll be quieter than mice, because let's face it, mice are not exactly silent with their squeaks and chirps and clawing and digging and gnawing."

Emily lifted her left hand beside her face, curling her fingers into tiny claws, and scrunched up her nose and cheeks in quick little wiggles. "But they are so cute, Sarah."

Sarah smiled. "Guess what I brought for my not very mousey

assistant? A croissant stuffed with pumpkin and cream cheese." She held up the bag from Java and Juice. "But don't mind me. I'll set up for the day. You do your thing."

Still in mouse mode, Emily grinned and made little biting sounds and movements. "Thanks, boss, you rock."

Sarah went to the dryer and started folding the towels from Saturday morning while Whiskey provided emotional support as Emily took her quiz by lying against her left ankle and sighing occasionally.

When the towels were all folded and stacked above the tubs, Sarah refilled the shampoo bottles from the gallon jugs stored under the sinks. Then she arranged all of the implements—clippers, scissors, combs, brushes, shedding blades, nail clippers, etc. at each grooming station. It was a bigger dog wash day, and, conveniently for Sarah, Katie Smith and her Samoyeds, Babs and Tabs, were the first customers of the day and Katie had promised to share what information she could from Paul Whitmore's rental application. Sarah drank black coffee from her to-go tumbler and picked at her croissant as she waited for them.

At eight o'clock, Sarah turned the closed sign to open and unlocked the Coiffure's green front door. Emily came out of the breakroom and grabbed the apron that matched Sarah's from a coat tree in the corner.

"How'd it go?"

"The croissant was killer, and I crushed the quiz. One hundred percent. Oh, yeah!" Emily pumped her fist in the air.

"You go, woman. That's awesome."

"I like this program so much, Sarah. It will add so much to the

Coiffure once we go into business together." Em's grin held promise, hope, and sass.

"It definitely will." Sarah had offered that when Emily became a certified pet nutritionist that they could turn one of the back rooms into an office and she could offer nutritional therapy and dietician services in addition to the grooming.

Just then the front door pushed open and Whiskey ran to greet his snow-white friends. Katie Smith trailed behind Babs and Tabs. Her super-model thin frame was covered in a charcoal gray pants suit with a finely knit silk turtleneck sweater underneath the jacket. Her black hair was sleek and straight in a bob that barely brushed her shoulders. Her hair had the precision cut Sergio was known for, and Sarah was envious at how her hair hung just so. Sarah's red tresses were reminiscent of sea kelp moving in the currents; her hair did what it wanted unless she harnessed its power with an elastic or a clip.

Babs and Tabs weren't tall or huge, but they were blessed with thick, fluffy double coats of fur. Sarah estimated the dogs weighed fifty pounds each, about the same weight as Whiskey. Because of their extra fur, she always allotted an extra thirty minutes for them in the schedule and she and Em would use every minute.

"Sarah, Emily. Good to see you both," Katie said. She let the dogs go from their leashes so they could romp with Whiskey, and he led them right under the hinged part of the counter and raced toward the back of the Coiffure with the Samoyeds giving chase.

"About the information you asked for, Sarah," Katie started, sliding a piece of paper across the counter. "Here are the names and numbers of his references. The background check showed previous addresses in Virginia and Boston. The employment check listed a twelve-year stint at one of those big consulting firms, followed by almost twenty at another. He wrote he was currently retired."

"What kind of consulting firms? Accounting? Governmental?" Sarah glanced down at the paper Katie had given her but only the references and phone numbers were on it. She didn't recognize any of the area codes.

"McKinsey and Accenture, to be specific."

"Huh. So he could have been in tech or finance or strategic operations or anything."

Katie nodded her head and not a single hair moved. Sarah wondered what was on it, keeping it shiny and still.

"Anything else that would be good for me to know?" Sarah asked. Behind her, Emily had scooped up Babs and was carrying her to the tub, as Tabs and Whiskey followed.

"One thing I didn't notice until I looked at the reports again this morning to see what I could share with you. Buried on the last page was a credit card account pulled years ago and never closed." Katie paused for beat and gazed at Sarah with a knowing glimmer in her eye, like she was about to hand her a prized diamond of a clue.

"Yes?" Sarah asked, the anticipation causing her stomach to bubble.

"The name on the account was Paul Buffalo."

"What?!" Emily's voice exploded above the gush of water running over Babs.

"I did not see that coming." Sarah's eyes were wide as a barn owl's in a flashlight beam, her mind already stitching together a dozen new possibilities that made the room feel suddenly smaller and sharper. "Does Chief James know?"

"No idea. I haven't called the police. They haven't asked me for the background checks or his rental application. And like I said, I just noticed it this morning, when I pulled the information for you. Crazy, huh?" Katie's red lips curved into a knowing smile. "I'm sure you'll want to talk to Bunky."

"Umm, yeah. As soon as I wash and groom Tabs, and all of the rest of the dogs today. Paul was a Buffalo? I never would have guessed. Thank you for pulling the paperwork and for being forthcoming. I appreciate it. I'll let you know what I find. Can you return for the girls around eleven?"

Katie glanced at her watch and then back up at Sarah. "Sounds good. I'm showing a couple a few houses this morning. I'll come get Babs and Tabs when I'm done."

Katie exited the Coiffure and Sarah grabbed Tabs and put her in the tub next to her sister, who was already lathered from head to tail.

"That's so crazy, Sarah. Do you think Paul is brothers with Bunky or cousins or what?"

"No idea, and I don't want to speculate."

Bunky Buffalo was infamous in their town for getting drunk on homemade hooch after his mama died and shooting things up—trees, the barn, tin cans, the fence—out on his property outside of Cottageville. He discharged his gun so many times and made such a racket that his neighbors called the cops. And when Officer John Beams responded, Bunky was so out of his head with drink and grief, that he brandished the gun at Beams, who was forced to stun-gun him for both of their safety. Bunky served no time, since the whole town felt sorry for him, but he was sent to rehab. Rumors were that the treatment didn't stick. But for the most part, Bunky kept to himself on his rundown farm.

Sarah didn't relish the thought of going out to his place to talk to him, especially since she didn't know him well. But she had questions, the type of questions one only asks when face to face. She ran through various scenarios and even more questions, like first and foremost, why and when did Paul change his name if he had actually been born with a Buffalo surname?

She rinsed the suds from Tabs' dense coats until the water ran clear, and then she wrapped the dog in a fluffy towel and carried her to the stainless steel table next to her sister, where Em was blow drying and brushing out enough loose fur to create a small pet. Sarah rubbed the towel all over Tabs, helping to absorb some of the moisture, before she, too, took up the brush and blow dryer.

After Emily placed Babs on the floor so she could once again gallop with Whiskey, she lifted the lid of her laptop and her fingers flew over her keyboard. She read and searched until Sarah was finished with Tabs and the dog was playing with the others. Sarah grabbed a broom and swept up the fur clippings and cleaned out hers and Em's brushes. When she was done, Sarah asked, "What'd you find?"

"A classmates website has old yearbook photos of Bernard Buffalo and his younger by two years brother or cousin Paul Buffalo. They weren't bad looking as teens."

Sarah smirked. "But you think they are now."

"One looks old. Or maybe tired is the right word. And, well, the other is a corpse, so...come here and see for yourself. I left the tab open."

Sarah walked to the table and looked where Em's finger touched the screen. "Bunky was certainly skinnier. His head and face look more bowling ball shaped now."

Em let loose one "ha," and said, "Bunky is much more fitting than Bernard. Way too formal for the guy we know. He and Paul looked nothing alike, not even back then except for the eyes, maybe."

"Maybe," Sarah agreed. "And the ruddy complexions. But you're right." She wracked her brain coming up with the names of the families who had been in Cottageville for generations. She was almost certain the McGowans were on that list as well as the Buffalos. Maybe Trish, or her father, who had served as mayor for a decade or more, would be able to help Sarah fill in some blanks. "Can you tell from anything if they were siblings or some other type of kin?"

"I haven't yet, but I'll keep looking."

Just then the Coiffure's front door opened and the three dogs barked and raced to greet the newcomer. Harlequin Great Dane Lilly, a one hundred and twenty pound beauty that always left Whiskey bumbling around her like a lovestruck pre-pubescent boy, came through the door, followed by one of her moms, Holly, who along with her wife owned the Whispering Pines Boutique B&B, Cottageville's only inn and its most celebrated and sought-after wedding venue.

With his tongue protruding from the right side of his mouth, Whiskey sat on his haunches immediately in front of the giant dog, who walked until she stood above him and then nuzzled her nose against his ear. He stretched his lips into his biggest cattle dog smile, while Babs and Tabs sniffed the newcomer's back legs and butt.

"Hey, Holly. How are you and Lilly today?" Sarah asked from the far side of the counter.

"Good. We had a full inn over the weekend. So many people were in town for the Halloween parade and festival."

"Ooo, too bad they didn't get to experience much of it. Did they find other things to do?"

"We ended up creating a pumpkin patch on the back lawn and a scavenger hunt for the younger kids and told ghost stories around a campfire and had a marshmallow roast and s'mores event for families on Saturday. Then yesterday, we set up bobbing for apples and a bunch of games during brunch before people had to check out and return home. It was a fun weekend."

"Oh wow. That's wonderful and it sounds like it. And quick thinking on your parts."

"We try to be prepared for anything... but never expected a murder to close down the festivities." Holly shook her head slowly.

"Did you know Paul?" Sarah asked, stepping aside as three of the dogs barreled under the counter and sped through the grooming area into one of the back rooms.

"He stayed with us for one night six or eight months ago, way before he moved to town."

"Really? Did he say then why he came to Cottageville?"

"Just that he had some business in the area. He kept to himself and didn't say much. Arrived right at check in and then left right after. I didn't see him return, but he did eat breakfast by himself in the dining room before checking out."

"Did he indicate he planned to return or to move here?"

"No, but Lisa and I once ran into him at the pizzeria. We were surprised to see him sitting at a table by himself when we walked in. We recognized him right away and Lisa said, 'Hi, Paul. We didn't know you were back in town.' That's when we learned he had moved here and rented Micas Brighton's house."

"Did he say why he moved here?"

"No. But we didn't ask. We just said stuff like, 'Welcome to Cottageville. We love having new neighbors. You'll love it here.'"

Sarah bit her lip debating if she should ask the next question. But she figured she had nothing to lose, so she said, "Did he act like he had lived here before?"

"What? No. I don't know. Why?"

"Um, because we think his last name may have originally been Buffalo and that his photo is in a Cottageville yearbook from… what's the date on that yearbook, Em?" Sarah said the last bit over her shoulder.

"The early 1980s," Emily said as she stepped forward and grabbed ahold of Lilly's collar and led her to a walk-in tub. Whiskey now trailed behind them, refusing to let Lilly out of his sight.

The Coiffure door opened again and Tabs and Babs ran to the door with the wispy ends of their hair flying to greet their human. Katie Smith knelt and wrapped her arms around her squirmy balls of love. "Oh girls, you look gorgeous and you smell so clean," she enthused, kissing the tops of their heads.

When she straightened to standing, she said, "Hi, Holly. Good to see you. Sarah, you and Em have outdone yourselves once again. My girls look fabulous. Thank you." Then she passed her black credit card across the counter so Sarah could complete the transaction.

"Two hours?" Sarah asked after Holly, who was waving from the door.

"Yes, two. Gotta go. Good talking to you, Sarah."

Sarah handed Babs and Tabs' leashes to Katie and then asked her, "How long have you lived in Cottageville?"

"A decade, give or take a few months."

"And why did you move here, if you don't mind me asking?"

"Not at all. I was working in a big city agency after I got my real estate license. You know, small fish, bigger pond and all of that. I heard through a friend of my parents that their long-term friend was the only real estate agent in this town and wanted to retire but needed someone to take his place. I did a little research and learned he really was the only broker in thirty-five miles, so I decided to give it a shot and here I am."

"And now you're a big fish in a small pond," Sarah joked.

"Exactly. Though Kristin Powers moved here a few years ago so I'm not the only fish anymore. But I haven't regretted moving here yet. Sure, the volume is lower than in a bigger place, but so is the cost of living, and my relationships are deeper and I'm happy to be *the* person people in Cottageville call when they want to buy, sell, or rent. It's good to feel needed and a part of the community."

Sarah beamed at her. "That's exactly how I feel, too."

"Well, I need to run and get these girls home. I've got a meeting in an hour on the outskirts of town and these dress clothes won't cut it and I don't want to be late. Thank you, Sarah. Have a good rest of your day."

"You, too."

Once again, Sarah wondered what brought Paul Whitmore to town... or back to town and maybe his final resting place. She shivered at that thought.

CHAPTER 9

Since Emily seemed to have Lilly's bath under control, Sarah pulled her phone from her apron pocket and dialed the mayor's phone number. Her assistant answered on the second ring.

"This is Sarah Carter. I was wondering if Mayor Trish had ten minutes for me to stop by any time this afternoon or tomorrow morning."

"She's out this afternoon. But would tomorrow at nine work for you?" the mayor's assistant asked.

Sarah checked their schedule. An older woman named Peg who dyed her hair to match the seasons was on the schedule at eight-thirty.

She had requested Emily color her white poodle's ears "like changing leaves" for autumn.

"Nine would work perfectly. And like I said, I only need a few moments. Thank you. See you then." Sarah disconnected and added the meeting to her phone calendar and the Coiffure's schedule. But of course, there was a chance she'd run into the mayor in the morning in Java and Juice and be able to talk to her there.

"Hey, Em, do you mind if I run over to the county clerk's office? I want to see if I can get a plat map for Cottageville and the surrounding areas." Sarah was already pulling her apron over her head before Emily even answered. She hung it on the hook and turned back to look at her assistant.

Em's eyes were wide and round like an anime character's. "You think Paul being here had something to do with land?"

"I don't know. But he was researching the town's history. Who owns, or did own, the land and businesses is part of that."

"Makes sense. I've got this. Just get back before Sebastian the St. Bernard gets here. Remind me why again we booked all of these bigger beasts on the same day. Do we never learn?" She stretched her sudsy hands overhead, before turning on the water to rinse Lilly while Whiskey supervised.

"I'll be quick. I promise." Sarah eased open the Coiffure door and then took off down the sidewalk at a brisk pace.The county clerk's office and the police station were a block from the far entrance of the library on the road that parallelled Main Street. Sarah said, "Hi," to people as she passed, but she never broke her stride, letting people know by her body language she didn't have time to talk, that she was on a mission.

Five minutes later, she pulled open the glass and steel door of the county clerk's office and greeted Martha, who had worked at the front desk for twice as long as Sarah had been alive. Martha wore a black cardigan over her big floppy bow at the neck white blouse and her silver beehive added five inches to her slight frame.

"Sarah. Great to see you, dear," exclaimed the seventy-six year old, who had no plans to retire. "Where's your furry sidekick?" Martha's drawn-on brows were raised.

"With Emily. She's washing Lilly and Whiskey won't be separated from her. Do you know Lilly? She's the Great Dane in residence at Whispering Pines."

"I have not had the pleasure," Martha said. "What can I do for you? Surely, this is not a social call." Her coral lips curved into a smile, showing a hit of lipstick on her front teeth.

"I would like a copy of the plat map for the area."

"A certified or non-certified copy?"

"Non-certified is fine. How much is it?" Sarah reached into the front right pocket of her jeans and pulled out some rumpled cash."

"Five dollars." Martha clicked some keys on her computer and Sarah heard a printer chatter to life.

Sarah slid a five dollar bill across the counter to Martha.

"Are you looking at anything in particular?"

"I am reading some Cottageville history books and they talked about some of the founding families and their land. I want to see how it's changed and how some of the big farms were broken up."

"Any specific ones? I've been here a long time and have

personally witnessed those changes." Martha's eyes sparkled when her smile reached them.

"Know anything about the Buffalo land?"

"I know developers have had their eyes on that land for decades. It's a few hundred acres. Three brothers originally settled here back in the day, in the eighteen hundreds, it would have been. Each one got about one hundred and fifty or one hundred and sixty acres to farm."

"Wow. That's a lot of land," Sarah interjected.

"Yes, but remember the average farm in Iowa at the 1910 census was one hundred and fifty-eight acres."

"I had no idea."

"So the Buffalo land was average." Martha smiled again showing her teeth and this time Sarah motioned for her to wipe her front tooth by saying, "You have a little something..."

"Thank you, dear. Anyway, those brothers farmed it and made a good living for a while. That would have been Bunky's grandfather and his brothers, that generation."

"But then came the wars and the droughts and all of the other calamities." Martha shook her head and her beehive didn't even wobble. "And the family was hit hard by deaths and other disasters."

"How many acres of the land is still owned by them?"

"It'll be on the map. My guess is maybe three hundred of the original acres. A few bits got sold off here and there."

Sarah's eyebrows hiked to almost her hairline. "So Bunky and any other Buffalo family member is land rich?"

"You know how the saying goes. Land rich and cash poor. That's been the family for far too long." Martha's eyes looked glassy like the comment pained her. "Bunky's mama was a good woman."

"Did she have any children besides Bunky?"

Martha shook her head. "No. God rest her soul. She almost died giving birth to him—started hemorrhaging. Her husband couldn't afford to lose her so they agreed one child would be enough. Of course, then he died not too many years after—a heart attack on the tractor one day—and left her a widow with a young son."

"I had no idea," Sarah said. She glanced at her watch and realized she had been talking to Martha for too long. "I'm sorry to cut this short but I've got to get back. Thank you for the chat and the plat maps, Martha. I really appreciate your help."

"Anytime, Sarah. Pat Whiskey for me and bring him next time."

"I will," Sarah said over her shoulder and she walked out the door. She jogged the whole way back to Rosewood Drive and the Coiffure.

Scott Simon's black Explorer pulled to the curb just as Sarah was opening her business's green door. She held it open while Sebastian lumbered from the vehicle and then towards her. Scott's salt and pepper hair was curly like a Kerry blue terrier's and he wore his standard uniform of cigar colored Blunstone boots, army green jeans, and a navy blue button down flannel.

"Hello, Sarah. Are you coming or going?" Scott asked.

"Returning after an errand. How are you today?"

"We are fine, though Sebastian has been slowing down." Scott frowned as ribbons of drool fell from Sebastian's jowls. "Sorry about the slobber."

"It's part of the breed," Sarah said with a smile. "We have plenty of towels. How old is he now?"

"Eight. I don't like to think about it."

"I understand. Whiskey is seven and a half. But cattle dogs live a bit longer than other breeds."

"Dr. Schank says his heart still sounds healthy, so maybe we'll have a couple more years. But he's slower and not as interested in walks and he just acts old. Know what I mean?"

"I do and I'm sorry. It's difficult to watch them age, and even more difficult if they are suffering." Sarah put a hand on his forearm. "He's a beautiful dog with a kind and gentle soul."

"Thank you, Sarah. Should I return to get him in two or three hours?"

"Yes, whenever it is convenient for you."

Sarah shut the door as Scott returned to his SUV.

"That was sad, Sarah. Very sad. I overheard most of it." Emily stood at the counter. Whiskey, Lilly, and Sebastian were in the waiting area sniffing each other and getting reacquainted.

"Sorry I was gone longer than I anticipated." Sarah set the plat maps on the counter and grabbed Sebastian by the collar.

Emily opened the hinged part of the counter for Sarah and Sebastian to walk through, and then she moved the maps onto a table in the back. "Hey, while you wash him, I'll scarf down my salad, and then both of us can tag-team on the blow drying and styling."

"Sounds good. Thank you." Sarah led Sebastian to a walk-in tub and the dog entered willingly. "Good boy," Sarah enthused, as she rubbed his ears. She shut the tub door and then realized she wasn't wearing her apron. "Hang on a second. I'll be right back."

She took ten measured steps to the rack, grabbed her apron, and slipped the loop over her head with the ease of habit. Wrapping the ties twice around her waist, she secured it snugly—just in time. The moment water hit Sebastian's thick coat, he exploded into action, twisting and shaking like a furry cyclone. A tidal wave of spray erupted, soaking everything in its path. Sarah flinched as warm droplets slapped her face, drenched her apron, soaked through her sleeves, and ran down into her tennis shoes. *Ah, the glamorous life of bathing big dogs,* she mused, blinking water from her eyes. She reached for the shampoo bottle, squeezing a generous dollop into her palm. With firm hands, she quickly began to work it into his broad shoulders, massaging the suds deep into his dense fur and moving steadily down his back.

Twenty-five minutes and four Sebastian shakes later, the water around the dog ran clear and Sarah was sure she looked like a proverbial drowned rat, if the rat had running mascara, drips falling from its nose and chin, and its shoes squished with each step.

Emily popped out of the break room and issued a "Holy crap. Were you in a wet dog groomer contest and didn't tell me? You dirty dog!"

"Very funny, smarty. Sebastian is fine with taking a bath. It's the being wet part he doesn't like."

"Hmm. You could be onto something here, Sarah. Dry shampoo for dogs. Sounds like a million-dollar idea." Em pulled her phone from her apron's pocket, snapped a quick pic of a not-amused-looking Sarah, and typed something in. "Darn it. It's been done. A lot apparently.

Why have I never heard of this? Why don't we have some? Sarah, it would save us from getting soaked."

Sarah walked Sebastian from the tub to the rectangular table almost built into the floor. Its legs were literally two inches tall. She rubbed the dog with a bath sheet as she responded to Emily. "Yes, but it is best for spot cleaning and in between cleaning, not for scrubbing dogs who get their jollies from rolling in… whatever it is they roll around in. Manure. Compost. Rotten eggs. And all of those disgusting things we get asked to fix."

The right side of Emily's mouth quivered "Rriiiiiigghhtt." She drew out the word into multiple syllables. "By the way, Rebecca Davis called while you were out. She said French Fry has been extra itchy and asked if we could fit him in this afternoon. I hope it is okay that I said yes. Bobby will bring him by when school ends. She said around three-thirty."

Em picked up a brush and stood on the opposite side of Sebastian from Sarah, waiting for the toweling to stop.

French Fry was a bichon frise who lived with nine-year-old Bobby and his parents, and Bobby was one of Sarah and Emily's favorite pet companions because he considered his dog his best friend. During the summer when he brought French Fry by for a bath, Bobby stayed the whole time and waited like a parent who couldn't stand the thought of leaving their toddler at daycare and out of their sight. But he wasn't neurotic or nervous. He sat quietly and ran his hands through Whiskey's soft fur, and told Sarah how his house had been robbed the night before and how sad that had made his mom. The information was delivered in the way only a child who didn't fully grasp the situation could: matter-of-fact and emotion-less except for the empathy for his mother.

"Did you see them at the pet parade? I thought Bobby said they'd be there and would dress up, but then I didn't see them."

"They were in the very front, after the marshal. French Fry was wearing a red box with that classic M on it filled with foam fries and Bobby was dressed as a ketchup bottle. It was hiilllllaaaarriiiiioouuss." Again, Emily stretched out the word and emphasized each syllable.

"Oh, wow. I hate that I missed that."

"Me, too. I couldn't even get my phone camera started quick enough and they were past me. Anyway, did you talk to Martha?"

"I did. And I learned that Bunky and Paul were not brothers. Bunky is an only child and his dad died when he was young."

"Oh, that's too bad. So who is Paul?"

"I don't know. A cousin? I'm hoping Mayor Trish might know. I made an appointment to see her tomorrow."

Sarah grabbed her own brush and turned on the blower dryer, prompting Em to do the same. They worked slowly and methodically from Sebastian's shoulders and legs down his ribcage to his back legs. When they were done, his coat gleamed like melted dark chocolate, soft and inviting, and he leaned into their hands with a sigh so content it felt like gratitude wrapped in fur.

"Awww," Emily expelled, wrapping her arms around Sebastian's neck. "I love you, too."

Whiskey slurped Emily upside the cheek, wanting in on the affection, and Lilly, who didn't want to be left out, leaned against Sarah, pushing her into Sebastian.

At that moment, a face appeared looking through the glass on the front door and then it opened. Holly called out, "I hope I'm not interrupting anything..."

"It's all good, a regular love fest," Em said, straightening up from her crouched position. "Your girl was so good today, so patient with her bath and blow dry. She's a sweetheart."

"Whiskey certainly thinks so," Sarah added with a smirk.

"Well, she loves all three of you." Holly set a card on the counter and Sarah ran it through their system.

"Hey, Holly, when Paul stayed with you, he didn't mention or meet with Bunky Buffalo, did he?"

Holly's brow furrowed and confusion creased her features, as if Sarah had just asked her to recite the periodic table backward. She blinked twice, then shook her head slowly, then asked, "Why would he?"

"Umm, well, we think they may be related."

"If they are, it is news to me. Thank you for making Lilly look her best. I've gotta run. Come on, girl." Holly clipped the leash to her dog's collar and they left the Coiffure.

As Holly and Lilly stepped out the front door, Emily turned to Sarah with a raised brow. "Wow," she said, "She really doesn't like being questioned, does she?"

"It appears that way, Em, but I think she is just more reserved and may not be interested in the details of Paul's life, or should I say death."

Em smirked, "Yeah, not everyone thinks like Sarahlock Holmes."

Two hours later, after Scott had picked up Sebastian, they had a few down moments while they waited for French Fry, their last client of the day. Emily started restocking the shampoo bottles and straightening the shelves of supplies to get ready for the following day, while Sarah picked up all of the wet towels they had used throughout the day and added them to the washing machine, which she then ran.

Sarah's phone sounded with a loud, "Na na na na na Batman!"

Emily quipped, "Really, Sarah?" as Sarah answered the call, "Hi, What's up?"

A few beats of silence passed where only the water entering the washing machine could be heard.

Then there was a one-sided conversation filling the Coiffure. "Where was it exactly?" Sarah bit her bottom lip with her top teeth.

"Did you call Chief James?" Her eyes narrowed.

"Was it like the other one?" She toed the floor with her still-wet sneaker and watched her foot move.

"Whiskey and I should be home around five." Sarah's green eyes met Emily's as if she knew her assistant was dying to know what was going on.

"We'll be fine. It doesn't seem like a threat. Just someone having some fun." Sarah held the phone from her ear a couple of inches on Jared's reply. Then she said, "Yes, I know I can't be certain. But we will keep our eyes peeled and take every precaution. I love you. Thank you for calling."

When she placed her phone back into her apron, Sarah said, "Well, someone made an effigy of me, too, and hung it from the street sign for my street at the edge of the park."

CHAPTER 10

"A *what*?" Emily screeched. "And what do you mean, too?"

"Yesterday, when Jared and I took Whiskey on his morning walk, we found hanging from one of the park lampposts—you know those big ones on the cement and stone pillars when you first enter the park from Main Street? Well, anyway, we found a small stuffed doll dressed in a police uniform and made to look like Chief James. I called him and had him come look at it in case it was...well... anything. It was cute and well-made but strange."

"A doll like a voodoo doll?"

"Not exactly. It was lacking the pins."

"How did you know it was Chief James and not Beams or another male officer?" Em asked.

"Whoever made it sewed his nameplate onto the uniform. It was 'Order'."

"Wow. Tiny details."

"Yep. And the one Jared found on the opposite end of the park had my red hair and green eyes and was wearing my Sherlock Halloween costume."

"Oh my God, Sarah. That's crazy! Someone made that this past weekend." Emily shuddered with a chill and rubbed her arms with opposite hands.

"They must have because no one but Jared knew what my parade costume was going to be until I put it on right here in the Coiffure bathroom."

"So whoever is making these things was at the parade."

"Most likely."

"And clearly knows how to sew."

"Yes."

"Did they look hand stitched or done on a machine?"

"I don't know. The main seams may have been on a machine, but the threads to form the nose and the tiny details like the police badge and name plate looked whip-stitched, if I remember correctly, the stitches Gigi taught me as a girl."

"I can't believe you didn't tell me about this," Emily mumbled, before teasing, "We're a team, Sarah. An investigative team."

"Sorry. It slipped my mind. The murder of Paul took precedence."

"Understandable. But still, now we have two mysteries to solve...

once again. I'm going to read up on effigies tonight after I finish my homework."

They halted the conversation since Bobby's big brown eyes peered at them through the glass.

Emily opened the door and flashed Bobby a big smile. "Hey, Bobby. How's it going? How's French Fry?" She tickled under the little white dog's chin, who was cradled in Bobby's arm like a football. Her pink tongue protruded from her mouth in a way that didn't make her look like the smartest dog in town, but she was definitely one of the cutest.

"We had a math test today. I don't like tests, but I like math better than spelling. Some words are hard."

Emily nodded her head. "Yes, some are. What's the hardest word you know how to spell?"

"We learned 'magnificent' last week so I know that one. But I missed 'opponent' on the quiz because I forgot the second p." Bobby frowned. "I don't much like opponents anyway. Everyone should get along. French Fry loves everyone, don't you, girl?" He nuzzled his nose against hers.

"You're right," Sarah said. "Life would be so much better if everyone got along. Is French Fry ready for her bath? Do you want to stay and watch? We can give you an apron and you can come back here and supervise. Is that a word you've learned to spell?"

"It isn't, but I know what it means, I think. And nah, I'll wait out here." Bobby handed French Fry to Emily and then he parked himself on the sofa, swinging his feet back and forth since they didn't touch the ground. He hummed a tune Sarah didn't recognize. Whiskey rested in sphinx pose on the floor of the waiting area where he could keep an eye on both the front door of the business and on Bobby.

Sarah offered to tag-team French Fry by washing one half of her while Emily washed the other, getting the bichon bathed in record time. On the grooming table, Sarah took lead on the trimming of the French Fry's body and tail while Emily worked on crafting the spherical ball of fur encasing the dog's head. This was the way Bobby preferred his dog. By the time they were done, the bichon frise stood proudly on the grooming table, its head transformed into a perfectly sculpted cotton ball—fluffy, round, and impossibly white, like a tiny cloud that had drifted down from a blue sky and decided to sprout a pair of black button eyes and a black nose.

"She's perfect!" Bobby exclaimed, leaping from the sofa and clapping his hands. Whiskey ran to him and circled him once, nudging right above his sneakers, like he was trying to herd Bobby's enthusiasm.

"Whiskey, it's okay," Sarah said. She carried French Fry through the hinged counter and handed her back to Bobby.

"Thank you, Sarah. Mom told me to ask you to run her card. Is that okay?" He fished a Visa card out of his front pocket and handed it to her. "Oh and she said to add ten dollars for the tip."

"Thank you." Sarah handed the card to Em, who was on the payment side of the counter.

When the transaction was completed, they gave the card back to Bobby and saw him and French Fry to the door. Bobby walked toward Main Street rubbing his cheek on the top of his dog's poofy head, which caused Sarah to chuckle. "They are the cutest," she said.

"Indeed. And we finished early. Good job," Emily said. "What will you do with this unexpected gift of time, Sarah?" The right side of Em's mouth curled upwards.

"I'll probably check in with Mrs. Jenkins and see how she's feeling. You?"

"Travis is at work until six or seven."

"You could surprise him at the salon." Sarah wiggled her eyebrows at Em.

"Yeah. Right. You know Sergio. He'd love that. Spontaneity isn't part of the salon, and I would never want to get Travis in trouble."

"Point taken," Sarah said before teasing, "You'll just have to stick to those sexy selfies."

"Shut up." Em smacked Sarah lightly on her arms. "We are so not going there." Emily grabbed her backpack and raced to the door, saying "Bye, Whiskey. See you *mañana*, Sarah."

Sarah locked the door behind Emily and then moved the towels from the washer to the dryer and made sure everything was ready for the next morning, including putting the fur dye at Emily's station for Peg's poodle.

Then Sarah grabbed her own backpack, turned out the lights, and locked the door behind her. With Whiskey by her side, they turned right on Main Street and walked north until they got to the park. Sarah gazed at the light post, making sure not other effigies had been added since yesterday. Then she and Whiskey walked the path until they stumbled upon Officer John Beams in his civilian attire walking Coco Chanel, a red and white corgi, on a designer leather leash. Whiskey trotted ahead of Sarah to greet his two friends, John with a staccato bark and Ms.Chanel with a sniff of her tailless behind.

"Hey, John," Sarah said. "What a beautiful afternoon." Sarah eyed the still colorful leaves on the park's trees.

"It is a good day, Sarah. But I did hear there was a doll with the likeness of you found a few hours ago."

"That's what I've heard."

"How do you feel about it?" John's hazel eyes searched hers.

Sarah shrugged before she joked, "It feels way less threatening than some of the things over the past couple of years. And maybe I should be honored that someone ranks me up there with the chief." Her laugh that followed was humorless and hollow.

"It's very odd, for sure. We aren't sure what to make of them yet," John admitted.

"I get that. Hey, not to change the subject but did you know Paul Whitmore might be a relative of Bunky Buffalo?"

"I did not know that. Why do you think so?"

Sarah told him about the information provided by Katie Smith and the yearbook photos Emily found. She also mentioned the Cottageville history books Paul had been reading at the library. "I've checked most of them out and I've been going through them. I had no idea until now that the Buffalos were one of the first families in the area."

"There's really been no reason to think about it." Like Sarah, John wasn't originally from Iowa but after college and a couple of years working for Chicago P.D., he sought a simpler—and maybe safer— life. "Have you learned anything else about his life?"

Before Sarah had a chance to answer, he added with force, "And you are sticking to his life, right?"

Sarah grimaced at his question but conceded that she had been. "You probably already know this, but he doesn't have much of a digital footprint. I learned more from Katie than I had with hours of internet searching."

John nodded his head. "His cell phone is missing."

Sarah craned her neck and tilted her head like Whiskey did when he was listening intently. "Know what kind?"

"Unsure. What we do know is we didn't find one on his person, in his vehicle, or in his house. That's the only thing we could tell had been taken."

"Did you call the number? Maybe it fell between the couch cushions or dropped from his pocket wherever they strung him up. Maybe it broke and he hadn't gotten the replacement. There are a number of possibilities."

"Yes, or whoever killed him stole his phone... to keep us from reading texts or looking at his calls or contacts."

"Also a possibility," Sarah said. "Why—"

John cut her off. "Because you have a knack for finding things... even when you aren't looking. When you and Whiskey are out and about, keep your eyes peeled for a phone. That would help us a lot. And remember, it could be anywhere."

"Umm, do you mind if I call Katie to get the number from his rental application? I want to call the number as I walk around."

"You can, but remember, it's been three days now. Its battery may be dead."

"Or if the killer took it, they may have turned it into a brick so you, one of Cottageville's finest, couldn't track it via location services." Sarah smiled to herself for thinking of that.

"That is a likely scenario, too." John looked at his shiny silver watch with the big blue bezel and said, "I need to get going. Good running into you, Sarah, and thank you for your help looking into Paul's life. Come on, Coco, let's go see your daddy." He tugged gently on the corgi's leash and headed on the path toward Main Street.

"Well, that was interesting," Sarah said to Whiskey as they walked to the far end of the park toward home. Before they crossed Park Street, Sarah stopped to inspect the sign post. One single brown sliver of yarn stuck to the metal pole at eye level. She wondered if it had come from her effigy or was a fly away from someone's cozy knit scarf. And if it was from the effigy, why hadn't it been bagged with the doll as evidence? Though evidence of what, Sarah was unsure.

CHAPTER 11

The next day, Sarah opened the Coiffure at eight since Jazmin the Yorkshire terrier was arriving at eight-thirty. Sarah stashed the lime cilantro shrimp green salads in the refrigerator for her and Emily's lunch and placed the two oversized spiced muffins stuffed with caramel apple compote on the breakroom table. She broke off a piece of hers while she waited for Emily and perused *The Cottageville Courier* online. The update article on Paul Whitmore's murder quoted Chief James as saying they were still investigating and following down every lead. He encouraged the public to call if they knew any information about Paul or regarding his death.

Nothing new there, Sarah thought.

A feature article on the inside of the paper highlighted all of the dog rescue places within a fifty-mile radius. Sarah was thrilled to see a paragraph on Daisy and Donovan's poodle rescue. Daisy and Donovan had such generous hearts and a willingness to take in the most challenging animals. At their farm was where Sarah and Gladys met close to a dozen poodles, and where Gladys found her two beautiful girls, Kahlo and Cassatt.

Sarah loved that their town's newspaper wrote about and printed more than the sensational stories; they celebrated the successes and the heart and people of the community.

Emily used her key on the front door as Whiskey beat a solo stampede to greet her. She wore a black knit turtleneck dress that hit three inches above her knees and her black combat boots. Her hair was still black and hung straight in the back, but as she came closer, Sarah noticed the front of Emily's hair was secured with a turkey barrette that looked like a five-year-old's drawing on one side and a male pilgrim on the other.

"Umm, interesting hair accessories, Em."

She giggled. "They are just so ridiculous. I couldn't help myself. I had to buy them."

Sarah grinned. "I can see how you'd feel that way. And Em, wow girl, those dresses are getting shorter by the day. Meow. You gotta be driving Travis bonkers."

Emily planted her right hand on her hip, cocked it to the side, and tilted her head dramatically. She drew in her cheeks, puckering her lips into an exaggerated duck face. "When you've got it, you've got it," she said, breaking into a laugh at her own silliness as she reached for the denim paw print apron.

"Seriously though, is that a new t-shirt?" Em asked as she was still gathering her composure.

Sarah wore an evergreen long sleeve shirt emblazoned with "Dogtrovert: A person who prefers spending time with dogs instead of people" on the chest. "Jared bought it for me. He saw it in an airport during some leg of his book tour."

"Oh nice. But I think you like people, too, Sarah."

"Some of them." Sarah flashed Em a smile. "And some of them more than others. Jazmin should be here any minute. But did you learn anything about effigies last night? I saw John Beams on Whiskey's and my walk home yesterday, and he said they can't find Paul's cell phone."

Emily slid her apron strap over her head and tied it around her waist and then she picked up the muffin Sarah had bought for her. She sniffed it before taking a bite. After chewing and swallowing, she exclaimed, "OMG that is good. So much cinnamon and squishy apples. It's divine." She took a swig from her coffee cup. "Okay, so an effigy—which can be made of clay or wood or bark or cloth or wax or anything really—is used to represent a significant figure, usually in a cultural or political context."

"But are they good or bad?"

"They can be either. People make ones of their enemies and then burn or hang them as a way to protest or make a statement, or there are effigies of revered people in places like Westminster Abbey. The one I found most interesting was Fiend from The Misfits. I didn't even know Fiend is considered a cultural effigy and The Misfits are one of my favorite bands. You know what they say, right?"

Playing along with Em's sass, "No, Em, what do they say?"

"Come on, boss, didn't your mom ever tell you, 'ya learn something new every day.'"

Rolling her eyes, Sarah said, "Get back to your findings, punk rock girl, and leave the comedy to the people at the Comedy Club."

"Geesh, so snippy. Okay, what was I saying? Oh yeah, I read that Native Americans have made a lot of effigies of birds and animals and put them on everyday objects. When you said the Chief James effigy was hanging on the lamp post, was it arranged as an actual hanging or was it dangling from there or attached to it? And what about yours?"

"The one of Chief James definitely had a noose around its neck. I only saw a photo of mine that Jared had taken." Sarah frowned trying to recall all of the details since she didn't study the image. "There may have been a noose around mine, too, but I'm not really sure. The tweed coat was buttoned up so that may have obscured it. I'll have to ask Jared to text me the photo."

"Please do. I'd like to see it. So the purpose of an effigy is often to ridicule the person or thing represented. Though the First Nations people created theirs with reverence."

"So someone could be making fun of me and the police? Is that what you're saying?"

"Possibly. Or it could be that it is saying you are both culturally significant." Emily took another bite of her muffin, as the six-pound Yorkshire terrier and her human Caroline Hunt came through the door. Caroline was rather large compared to her tiny dog and was in her mid-sixties. She seemed to be in a perpetually good mood and she loved colorfully patterned dresses. Today's was an abstract design of oranges and purples with billowly sleeves and a midi length skirt. Her hair framed her round face in soft, silver-streaked waves with a will of their own—pinned up neatly at the crown, except for a few cheeky strands that escaped like teenagers sneaking out past curfew. The playful disobedience in those wisps gave her an almost conspiratorial charm, as if her hair knew a good joke she hadn't told yet.

Sarah's face lit up upon seeing them and she met them at the counter, picking up the small blue and tan dog. "How are you today, Jazmin? Is your mom treating you well?" she asked.

"Of course," Caroline said. "She's more spoiled than a gallon of milk left for a day in the sun."

"Eww," Emily said. "That's quite the picture."

Caroline's guffaw filled the Coiffure. "Honey, my language is intentionally as colorful as my clothes. You gotta have fun in all parts of life, otherwise, what's the point?"

"Wisdom," Em said.

"Thanks. Now, I must be on my way. I have a cutie waiting for me at the cafe and I don't want to be late." With that, she turned and shuffled out the door.

"A burst of energy," Sarah said. "I'll take care of Jazmin. Don't forget you have a wash and color coming at nine."

"It's Peg again, right? That poor poodle of hers. You know I'm all about hair expression, Sarah. But when people impose that onto their animals..." Em's voice trailed off.

"I agree. But I also feel like we are saving Patty from toxins and her owner doing something uneducated that is dangerous, like using paint or a product with bleach." Sarah put Jazmin in a wash tub and had her all wet and sudsy in under two minutes. Bathing a small dog was quick, and if the dog was cooperative, easy.

"True. I'm just not sure Patty likes it."

"Maybe we can talk Peg into doing just her tail or maybe her tail and the tips of her ears."

"I'll try. Are you still going to see Mayor Trish at nine?"

"Yes. She and Barbara weren't at Java and Juice this morning. I shouldn't be long."

Twenty minutes later, Peg had dropped off Patty and had agreed to Emily dyeing only the poodle's tail and the ends of her ears. Sarah had trimmed the shaggy fringe from Jazmin's coat and brushed her until she shined. Sarah made a ponytail at the crown of the Yorkie's head and added a small, burnt orange bow. Then she set the dog on the floor so she could curl up with Whiskey.

To Emily, Sarah said, "I'll be back soon," as she hung her apron from the rack and walked out the door. The morning was blue sky and white clouds but windy. The constant breeze stirred the falling leaves into a lazy ballet, each swirl and dip tracing quiet arcs across the sidewalks as if the trees were whispering their last stories before winter claimed the stage.

Sarah waved across the street to Daniel, who owned Buck and Son Hardware and who was engaged to and lived with her BFF Ginger. He was helping someone load a folding ladder into the back of a Subaru.

"Where's Whiskey?" Daniel asked across the few cars passing them on Main Street.

"At work. I'm running a quick errand."

Daniel nodded his head in understanding before saying something Sarah couldn't hear to the Subaru owner. Sarah didn't break her stride as she headed north on Main Street, crossed toward the library, and then walked another block to the city offices. She entered the door next to the county clerk's office and was surprised to see Mayor Trish in the front room instead of in her office. Her assistant wasn't at her desk.

"Hey, Sarah," the mayor said. She wore a navy jacket with a white button down shirt over a navy skirt.

"Hi. Thank you for seeing me. I have a couple of questions that I thought you might be able to answer, since your family has been in Cottageville for a very long time."

"We have. Almost since the beginning. Would you like to sit down?" Mayor Trish motioned to the leather chairs against the far wall.

"No, thank you. I know you are busy, so I will keep this short," Sarah said. "So you've known the Buffalos all of your life?"

"Pretty much."

"I know he's older than you, but have you known Bunky for most of the time?"

Mayor Trish smiled. "We aren't close, but it is a small town so I've known him and his mother. What's this about, Sarah?"

"I found some evidence that Paul Whitmore was originally named Paul Buffalo and that he went to Cottageville High School many years ago."

Mayor Trish's lips pressed into a straight line, a thin, wordless barrier that revealed more than speech could—equal parts restraint and quiet disapproval, or so Sarah thought. She waited for the mayor to respond.

After a few seconds of silence, she said, "I vaguely recall a mention of a Buffalo cousin called Paul. I think there was some kind of scandal with either him or his mom or dad…" Her eyes squinted and her face looked strained, as if trying to remember was physically challenging. "An affair or a pregnancy or some kind of swindle, that's what is coming to me, but I was so young at the time I'm not even sure I understood. And you know how rumors are, how even a kernel of truth can be lost in each whisper or telling. Or I could be remembering it incorrectly. All I do know is that it has been at least two decades since anyone who was born a Buffalo other than his mom and Bunky has lived in this town."

"Except maybe for the two or three months that Paul was here." Sarah's voice was barely above a whisper.

"If he really was kin," Mayor Trish said.

"Thank you for your time. I appreciate it." Sarah reached out her hand to shake the mayor's.

"That's all you wanted to know?" Trish clasped her hand and pumped it a couple of times.

"Yes, that was it. I needed someone whose family was one of the founders. Someone who knows the history of this place and its people."

"Anytime, Sarah. See you at Java and Juice in the morning."

Sarah smiled.

Eight minutes later, back in the Coiffure, Emily asked, "Did you learn anything?" Jazmin sat on the grooming table looking resigned and helpless.

Sarah went through the hinged part of the counter and gave the poodle a scratch behind her not-yet-dyed ear. Emily was working on the dog's tail.

"That Paul was most likely Bunky's cousin. Mayor Trish thought it was most likely a couple of decades since he lived here and that maybe some kind of scandal caused him or his part of the family to leave. But she couldn't remember what as she was too young."

"Well, something must have made him come back to Cottageville. And there must have been a reason he was reading all of those history books. Sarah, do you think there's a buried treasure somewhere? I heard on a podcast about some guy who buried a treasure and wrote a book and how all of these people have been looking for it for years and no one has ever found it. What if it is something like that? That would be so cool." Emily's enthusiasm increased as she talked. Her hands moved rapidly and she started bouncing on the toes of her Doc Marten's. "Think of it, Sarah, we could use our sleuthing powers to solve a mystery that isn't a crime. And it could make us rich."

Sarah chuckled. "Slow down there. You're as amped up as Elmo. Don't forget, a man was already killed for whatever it was he was trying to find and in a pretty dramatic fashion. I don't want us to be next."

Emily's feet were flat on the ground now and some of the excitement had left her eyes. "Way to be a buzz kill. Oops, I said kill. Hee hee. Don't mind me, Sarah. I've had way too much sugar and caffeine this morning, and this art project is driving me crazy. Why can't we just tell Peg no? No, you shouldn't color your canine and you shouldn't ask us to do it either."

"Like I said before I left, because I think she'd do it anyway... and we can prevent that from happening. This isn't ideal, but it is a compromise. Just like it was on Valentine's Day and for the Fourth of July. And I really, really appreciate you doing this. You have a knack. Look at how you do your own hair. I've admired it since I've known you."

"Gee, thanks, Sarah. But back to Mayor Trish, did you learn anything else?"

"Nah. But I'm not sure she knew Paul Whitmore was the same person as Paul Buffalo that she knew of back in the day."

"I wonder who did know that? Someone in town must have."

"I assume Bunky—" Sarah started but Em cut her off with a laugh, "Don't assume, Sarah, you know what that means."

Sarah smiled. "I do. I didn't make it to Bunky's yesterday to talk with him. Maybe I can go today."

Em shivered. "Don't go by yourself. Take Jared with you and Whiskey. It's a bit creepy being out there with only a couple of neighbors."

"It's more run down than creepy. But to your point, I definitely won't go alone." Anything else Sarah wanted to add was interrupted when petite Kristin Powers opened the door so Pedro, her Great Pyrenees, who was almost double her weight, could saunter inside.

Whiskey ran then slid across the floor to greet his massive friend.

Kristin stepped to the side so she wouldn't be knocked over like a bowling pin by Whiskey.

"Sorry about him," Sarah said. "How are you today?"

Kristin was dressed in an impeccable black pantsuit that seemed custom made for her size zero, four-foot-eleven-inch frame. She handed Sarah Pedro's leash. "I'm okay. Katie and I have been competing to be the primary realtors on this land development deal, and I'm not sure it is going my way."

"Where's the land?" Sarah asked.

"Out off the state route. A couple hundred acres."

"What are they building?"

"Subdivision mainly."

Sarah's eyes widened. "Won't there be enough places to sell for both of you?"

"You'd think. But the developer is from out of state and isn't doing things the way we do them around here."

"Well that sucks. Seems like it would be better to join forces. Where do they think all of the buyers are coming from? It isn't like this is a fast growing city."

"I know. But it's close enough to the city...at least that's how it will be marketed. Anyway, I have another meeting with them that I need to get to ... and I need to use a lint roller to get some of this dog hair off me. Can you hold Pedro until I return?"

"Absolutely,"

"Thank you, Sarah."

Sarah led Pedro, a cross between a gentle giant and an animated blond shag rug, into the walk-in tub. Something Kristin said was just out of reach in her mind, like a soap bubble drifting away on the breeze—close enough to see glimmering, but impossible to catch before it burst.

She turned the water on and thought about the effects of adding four or five hundred new houses to the area and all of those new people, probably at least two per home. *How many houses could be put on a couple of hundred acres? That would be enough to build a small, but high-density town. Who would that benefit and how? Besides the obvious financial gains.*

At that thought, Sarah wished she had asked exactly where the land was. She tried to envision the plat map. Where around town was there that much buildable acreage?

CHAPTER 12

Over a spaghetti and meatball supper, Sarah asked Jared, "Do you know anything about land development?"

He had a cherry tomato from his salad halfway to his mouth and paused his fork. "What kind of anything?"

"Let's say some company wants to buy some farm land or woods or whatever and create a subdivision. Do you know what steps they have to go through to do that?"

"First they'd have to buy the land from whomever owns it." He shoved the tomato between his lips and chewed.

"Do studies have to be done? Do drawings have to be filed? I'm sure they need some kind of permits." Sarah's eyes narrowed on her plate though she didn't really see the food.

"Yes, I'm sure. But you know what, you could go back and see Martha and I'm sure she could walk you through the process, or we could just ask AI for an overview." Jared's dimple was prevalent in his grin.

"You're so logical sometimes. It's weird for an artist." Sarah laughed.

Jared rolled his eyes and twirled his fork in the spaghetti.

"Would it be okay if I used my phone to look this up? I don't want to seem rude or distract from dinner."

"Go for it. Otherwise your brain won't be here at the table with us anyway." He put the forkful of pasta into his mouth and chewed. "I really like how this sauce turned out. It has just the right amount of kick from the pepper I added."

"It is really good, babe." Sarah asked her search engine for the developers legal requirements and process. She put down her fork and read aloud to Jared, "Says a title search must be conducted to show clear ownership, no liens, and the boundaries. Then there needs to be an environmental study to check for wetlands, floodplains, endangered species, etc. Followed by a feasibility study to look at market demand, infrastructure access such as roads and utilities and schools and to look at the estimated costs. Gees, Jared, that's all in step one."

"But it all makes sense."

"Most definitely. Step two looks like ensuring the property is zoned for residences and if not then an application for rezoning must be filed. There also has to be a comprehensive plan compliance review to make sure the subdivision fits into the city's long-term land-use plan. And that's when they have the public hearings about the proposals."

"I've never been to one of those," Jared said. "Have you?"

"Nope. But if someone wants to build a subdivision in Cottageville, I'd want to go. I'm not sure I like that idea."

"It could change the vibe of the town."

Sarah nodded her head, her eyes still on her phone. "Step three a preliminary plat has to be created and filed. Next is a review from city engineers to look at sewage and stormwater systems, road widths, fire hazards, and sidewalk plans. And then once the necessary changes are made, the plat map gets a final approval and is recorded with the county. After that it is pulling permits and getting approvals from utility providers. Followed by installing infrastructure like roads, sidewalks, sewer lines, and storm drains. And getting performance bonds to guarantee the work gets done. Then, they can finally get the building permits and start building the homes."

"Sounds like it takes a lot of time, some good lawyers and architects, and a lot of red tape. Want to tell me why you are suddenly interested in land development? You didn't inherit some fortune and didn't tell me, did you?"

Sarah giggled and set her phone aside, face down. "No, no instant wealth. Kristin Powers brought Pedro in today and mentioned she and Katie were competing to be the sales people for a new development."

"Do you mean like a subdivision or a commercial space?"

"Subdivision. She said it was at least a couple hundred acres."

Jared whistled. "Whoo-ee that could be a lot of houses and new people. Where might it be?" He speared a meatball with his fork.

"I'm not sure. She said outside the town off the interstate, I believe. But she wasn't very specific and I didn't ask."

"Could you imagine what our lives would be like if our population increased instantly by twenty-five, fifty, or even one hundred percent?"

"Traffic would be a mess. Our one-stop light and two lane roads weren't built for that."

"That's true. And we'd need more police, fire, and ambulance crew—besides just the Parks—and more teachers and bigger schools. We'd probably need another gas station than the one that we have, or it would need to expand from only two pumps. The hospital would need to have more staff." Jared's brow furrowed as he ticked through the list, the weight of practicality settling over his features, though a spark of curiosity lingered in his eyes—like he was half-wondering who on earth would ever want Cottageville to grow that fast in the first place.

Sarah silently ate the rest of her spaghetti and then finished her salad. "Hey, I meant to ask you, that effigy of me, did it look like it had a noose around its neck like the Chief James effigy did?"

"Maybe, or it could have just been the string that tied the doll to the pole."

"The one around Chief James' neck was braided and ochre in color."

"To be honest." Jared slid his hand across the table and placed it over top of Sarah's. "I didn't pay attention that closely. Yours had that tweed Sherlock jacket with the collar and I was so shocked by the sight of it, I didn't look for the noose. I saw it and it registered in my brain what it was and I called the police immediately."

"But you also took the photo." Sarah caressed Jared's fingers.

"I did, because I knew you'd ask what it looked like and want to see it.That's why people here call you Sarahlock."

Sarah's lips were caught between a smirk and a grimace. "I wonder who the next lucky person chosen to be an effigy model will be."

"I doubt we'll have to wait long to find out, assuming it wasn't planned for just the two of you." He squeezed her hand.

"Let's clean up the dishes and join Whiskey on the couch. I need some time with something funny, something to give my brain a break."

"Sounds good." Jared picked up both of their plates and Sarah followed with the silverware and the container of parmesan cheese. Jared put the leftovers in the refrigerator.

Just as they were walking into the living room, their doorbell rang. Whiskey almost knocked into them on his race to answer the door. Both Jared and Sarah went after him.

Officer Candace Grimes stood on the front porch. "Hey, Sarah, Jared, Whiskey. Sorry to bother you, but Bill, Gladys, and Janice ate at the Italian restaurant next door to the Coiffure tonight. When they came out, they found this hanging from your door knob, Sarah. Candace held up an evidence bag that contained an effigy of Jared, with a small paper copy of his graphic novel in one hand and to-go cup of coffee in the other. His little doll wore jeans and a forest green t-shirt and the maker had drawn in his beard scruff by using a fine tipped brush dipped in burnt sienna paint. Jared pointed that out to Officer Grimes.

"The likeness is incredible," he said. "Such attention to detail. The replica of my book cover is almost spot on."

"Ahh, but you're much more handsome," Sarah said, wrapping her hand around his arm. To Candace, she asked, "You said Bill, Gladys, and Janice found this?"

Candace nodded. "Janice spotted it and walked over to investigate. They didn't touch it. Bill called us and they waited until I got there. I brought it here because I wanted you to see it, and to know, Sarah, that it was intentionally left at your place of employment. We still don't know if this is someone's way of admiring people or if it is a threat. I didn't see cameras outside the Coiffure. Did I miss them?"

"No," Sarah said. "Our house is completely wired with constant video feeds. The business has a security system and a motion sensor light and camera on the backdoor, but none on the front. Rosewood Drive is high enough traffic I figured I didn't need one. Plus there's nothing to steal if someone breaks in other than towels and shampoo and scissors."

"I just thought that with the problems you've had in the past..." Candace's voice trailed off.

Sarah chose to ignore the comment and changed the subject. "Does it have a noose?" Sarah craned her neck to look more clearly in the evidence bag. She couldn't tell the answer to her question with the way Candace held the bag.

"I don't think so or maybe yes. The strings that attached it to the door knob were around its neck, but I didn't get a lynching vibe from it." Candace stared at the bag and the doll as if she was trying to see if her initial impression was incorrect. Her eyes squinted and her lips tightened in concentration, as if she were dissecting the details, Sarah thought, piece by piece—studying the stitching, the knot of the strings—searching for intention hidden in the craftsmanship rather than the shock value.

"I appreciate you bringing it by and letting us know," Jared said. "Someone is super artistic and very talented."

"I'm glad you admire their handiwork," Officer Grimes said, "but until we know if these are threats, you may want to pay attention to your surroundings and people at all times."

"Roger that," Jared said, to which Sarah rolled her eyes.

"You're watching too many cop shows. Now you're talking like Bosch," she said.

"Hey, that's a good show. I'll be back in touch if we learn anything else. Thank you for your time." Candace touched the front of her hat and returned to her car at the curb.

When Jared shut the front door, Sarah said, "You were right when you said we wouldn't have to wait long. Since they've done Chief James, me, and now you, I wonder if Whiskey and Sascha are next." A twinkle was in her eye.

"You may think I'm nuts, but I kinda want my mini-me once the mystery is solved. And the person is really good. That's the kind of assistant I need to help with the ink and color of my drawings in the new book."

"Let's find out if the person has criminal intent before you think of offering them a job," Sarah said.

Jared wrapped his arms around her and squeezed. "I love you so much."

"Aww, and I love you. Do you think I should call Bill or Janice or Gladys and ask them about finding the mini-you?"

Sarah could feel Jared's chin on the crown of her head moving back and forth in a no.

"You and Whiskey will visit Bill in the morning, like you do every morning. Ask him then. Right now, let's watch something lighthearted and then go to bed. Three-thirty will be here before I know it. Come on, Whiskey. I'll race you to the sofa." Jared let go of Sarah and sprinted toward the living room with Whiskey—as it was bred into his DNA—nipping at his heels in fun.

"I won!" Jared yelled, collapsing on the couch.

Whiskey jumped onto his lap and planted his butt so that he was facing Jared. Then Whiskey slurped his tongue from Jared's jaw to his hairline.

"You won a slobbering dog kiss, apparently." Sarah laughed and then cuddled next to them and picked up the remote.

CHAPTER 13

The next morning, Sarah donned a navy blue sweatshirt with a white portrait of a cattle dog with the words "Side Eye Society" above the image and army green cords. She put her auburn waves in a high ponytail and shoved her feet into fleece-lined boots since the ground was covered in frost. She carried her empty to-go tumbler and Whiskey's leash, though he wasn't attached to it. He trotted ahead up the sidewalk to the park.

Sarah said hello to Mrs. Jenkins, who had stepped out onto her front porch to pick up her newspaper from the welcome mat. She waved at Robert Wise as he slid into his Volkswagen's driver's seat to head off to school. As she and Whiskey crossed Park Street to enter

Cottageville Park, her eyes scanned the light poles and anywhere else an effigy could be tied. She didn't want to overlook any clues.

As they followed the path, Sarah found herself humming an old U2 tune, "I Still Haven't Found What I'm Looking For," before her awareness of what she was doing caught up to her actions, and she stopped mid-hum with a dry laugh. Too on the nose, she thought.

Whiskey's nose was to the ground sniffing an invisible trail, which Sarah guessed may have been by a squirrel, since he chased the scent toward the evergreen that was lit annually on December 1.

Sarah's gaze darted from lamppost to bench to the low branches of a maple, her detective's mind layering suspicion over ordinary scenery. A jogger Sarah didn't know passed with earbuds in and a young mom pushed a stroller with a fussy baby who was bundled with more layers than a burrito, but to Sarah it all felt like a stage set—waiting for the curtain to rise on something no one else had noticed yet.

A flash of fabric fluttered near the swingset, and Sarah's pulse quickened. She blinked, half-expecting another doll with its noose, but it was only a scarf caught on in the chain. Still, the jolt reminded her how thin the line was between the ordinary comforts of Cottageville and the strange shadows creeping in at the edges.

She wondered if the person or persons who had killed Paul did so to silence or stop him in particular or was it more random and not their first or last act of violence. The thought settled heavy in her chest, darkening the bright autumn morning. If it was targeted, then Paul had known something dangerous—something worth killing over. But if it was random, then Cottageville wasn't just sitting on a single crime; it was standing in the path of someone who could strike again.

She glanced down at Whiskey, who had returned to her and padded along beside her with his ears pricked, nose twitching at every scent on the breeze. "What do you think, boy?" she murmured. "Was Paul a target because of something he knew... or did we just stumble into a mess that's bigger than him—and bigger than us?"

Whiskey gave a low woof, as if answering, and flicked his tail once before resuming his steady trot.

Sarah sighed. "Yeah, that's what I'm afraid of, too. If someone's out there choosing victims at random, we're all in trouble. And if it wasn't random..." She shook her head, her voice dropping lower. "Then we have a killer who isn't finished yet. At least maybe."

When they got to the Main Street park exit, Whiskey automatically turned right on the sidewalk and sped up Bill's steps. Today he wore his black glasses partly down the bridge of his nose as he scanned the newspaper spread on the table in front of him. He had on a blue and gray plaid flannel shirt over navy track pants and thick wool socks. "Good morning, Sarah. Whiskey, so good to see you again. Give me five, dog."

Bill held out his hand and Whiskey tapped it with his right paw. "Good boy."

He handed Whiskey a beef dog biscuit. "I had no idea someone was putting effigies around town. Why didn't you tell me, Sarah?"

"I wasn't sure it was my place. The first we found was of Chief James. Jared and I found that one together. And no one knew what to make of it. Jared found the second one when he was by himself. Again, it didn't exactly seem threatening. But he called the police nonetheless. And then Janice and you and Gladys discovered the third.

Officer Grimes came to show us it in the evidence bag. Jared was acting more flattered and impressed with the artistry than he was disturbed." Sarah shrugged. "I have no idea what to think about those. Do you?"

Bill took a sip of his coffee before he said, "I remember during the Vietnam protests, people made much bigger ones of political figures and burned them. At least one group burned President Nixon's likeness and another President Johnson's."

Sarah nodded her head. "Yes, I know people do that during protests, but these little dolls haven't been burned and they aren't showing up with pins in them like voodoo dolls. And someone is clearly taking time and care to make the things and get all of the details right."

"That is true. The detail to Jared's book cover was almost an exact replica."

"Exactly, so it feels like..." Her voice trailed off. "Admiration seems like a strange word but that's what is coming to me." Then she frowned. "Though I'm still not sure if the rope around Chief Jame's doll's neck was meant to be a noose or not. It looked like it."

"That isn't good. Sarah, I'm glad we had that security system installed at your house and the cameras. It's always better to be safe than sorry, as cliche as that sounds. Until Chief James and his people get to the bottom of it, promise me you'll keep Whiskey nearby and your eyes open as you walk around."

"Of course I will, Bill. I appreciate your concern. And hey, I meant to ask you, is Janice really okay? Her health, I mean."

"She is. All of her bloodwork and scans came back fine except that her body didn't have enough sodium because she was overly hydrated. They gave her electrolytes and even some pretzels." He chuckled at that. "And that helped her recover."

"That's such great news."

"It really is. And Glad and I were thrilled that's what it was. I mean, that could be serious and life-threatening if not caught, but it was caught early enough. And it is much better news than a brain tumor or other things that can cause her symptoms. We feel very blessed."

"And I feel blessed to have you three as friends...well, actually you're more like family...without any dysfunction." Sarah giggled and then her face broke into a huge smile, the kind that stretched ear to ear and lit her features from the inside out, crinkling her eyes into half-moons and flashing teeth in a way that left no doubt about the joy behind it.

"Aww, we feel the same about you and Whiskey." Bill half stood from his chair so he could hug her.

Whiskey leaned against both of their legs to get in on the affection.

"I should be getting on my way. Thank you for Whiskey's treat and the conversation."

"Have a great day, Sarah."

"You, too."

Sarah and Whiskey waited until Main Street was clear of cars before crossing and then walking the half-block to Java and Juice. The bell tinkled on the inside of the red door as Sarah opened it. The scent of pumpkin and spices wrapped around her like a cozy quilt, warm notes of cinnamon and nutmeg mingling with the earthy bitterness of fresh-brewed coffee. It was the kind of aroma that made her shoulders drop a notch, signaling safety and comfort—even as her mind stayed busy with shadows and questions.

Some acquaintances waved over their morning pastries or breakfasts. Sarah smiled at some people and nodded her head in acknowledgement of others. She said to Mayor Trish and Barbara that she'd catch them on her way back out the door.

There was no line at the register so Whiskey marched himself to the counter and stood on his hind legs, with his toes touching the wooden top.

"Get down, boy," Jared said, tossing him one of Ginger's homemade chicken bone-shaped biscuits.

He caught it in the air and returned all four of his feet to the floor.

Sarah took his space at the counter and leaned over it to give Jared a quick peck on his lips. "How's your morning going?"

"Good. Steady but not crazy busy. Ginger made maple pecan eclairs for one of the seasonal pastries today. They are perfect. You should get those for your breakfast, and she made radicchio, pumpkin, and chicken salads with a tahini dressing on the side that is like an autumn explosion for your tastebuds."

"Yum. I'll take two of each." She handed him her to-go cup and he filled it with the dark roast house blend and bagged up the salads and eclairs. She ran her card through the reader, kissed him again, and said she'd be home around five-thirty.

As Sarah turned to leave, an idea struck her. She pivoted and leaned close to Jared hoping no one else could hear her. "Hey, do you have time to go see Bunky Buffalo with me after work today? I'd like to ask him a few questions, if he'll talk with us?"

Jared's green eyes seemed to grow bigger at her question, as if it wasn't what he was expecting her to say or ask. But then he said, "I can't tonight. I'm supposed to game with the guys. Can we go on Friday after work or over the weekend?"

"Yes, I guess so. I've been meaning to go for a few days..." She didn't finish her thought because as soon as that was out of her mouth, Jared cut in with, "Please, Sarah, do not go by yourself. It's not that I don't trust him, but it's way out there and anything could happen. I promise I'll go with you. It just won't be today."

"Okay. Thank you." She pecked his lips one more time.

When she and Whiskey passed by Mayor Trish and Barbara's table by the door, Sarah asked, "How are you ladies this morning?"

"Good, Sarah," Mayor Trish said.

Clad in her usual morning uniform of a form-fitting yoga top and tights, Barbara said, "I hear you and Jared are as lucky as my Jim, having little dolls made in your likeness. Someone must think you're special." She cracked herself up at her comment, but neither Trish nor Sarah laughed.

"Oh come on," Barbara continued. "They are great replicas, and it isn't like someone made them gruesome or macabre for Halloween. There were no protruding axes or swords, no fake blood, no intestines spilling out."

"Uh, no." Sarah said at the same time Mayor Trish said, "Thank God. We don't need that on top of one very real murder."

Sarah whispered, "Was the cause of death hanging or something else? Do you know?" She kept her eyes glued to Mayor Trish, willing her to answer.

Mayor Trish leaned closer to Sarah and Barbara did, too. The mayor said, "He was definitely hanged. Toxicology is still pending, but the medical examiner thinks he had a strong dose of sedative in his system before he was strung up. But you didn't hear that from me."

"From me, either," Barbara joked.

Mayor Trish patted her BFF's arm.

Sarah wondered if only coffee was in Barbara's cup. She had always been brash and sassy, but today she seemed over the top.

"Thank you for telling me," Sarah said. "Well, we need to go open the Coiffure. Barbara, maybe we can get Sascha and Whiskey together for a playdate soon. Mayor Trish, lovely talking to you as always. Enjoy the rest of your day."

As Sarah walked down the block and passed Produce and More and then got near the front of Buck and Son Hardware, she noticed a little fabric shape tied to the fire hydrant. Whiskey started to lift his leg to pee, and Sarah yelled, "No, Whisk, don't," and pushed his body around about forty-five degrees so he ended up dribbling on the sidewalk.

Sarah knelt down and eyed the doll in front of her, as she reached into the back pocket of her jeans and pulled out her phone and called Chief James.

When he answered with, "What have you found or discovered, Sarah?"

She replied, "A miniature John Beams, sir. And he's holding a teeny, tiny gun with his finger on the trigger."

CHAPTER 14

After relaying her location, Sarah agreed to stay put and guard the scene until he got there.

Once she disconnected with the chief, Sarah texted Em, "Please open the Coiffure. I found another doll and am waiting for the police. I'll be there as soon as I can. Thank you."

Emily responded, "Already here."

Sarah was glad her only employee was an early bird like she was.

Chief James arrived at the scene eight minutes later and Sarah spent that time keeping Whiskey away from the hydrant and trying to block the evidence from the few people who passed by who might have been curious.

Whiskey high-tailed it to Chief James for a head scratch as soon as his cruiser stopped at the curb. "Good morning, Whiskey. Sarah. You do have an uncanny way of finding things." Chief James' uniform was pressed and clean, exactly like it was on his effigy.

The uniform on the Officer Beams effigy wasn't quite as pristine. It looked more like John did after a full day of policing: mostly clean but with his shirt not as severely tucked into his pants and his tie a little askew. Sarah said, "Jared was right. The maker has such realistic attention to details. And clearly knows us all, and well."

Chief James took photos with his phone before donning gloves and gingerly removing the doll from the yellow hydrant's pent nut. When he turned the doll face down, Sarah gasped. "Isn't that a taser holder on the left back hip of the belt?"

"It is. And it is exactly where John carries his. It goes on the nondominant side so you never confuse it with your firearm."

"So the maker knows John is right handed."

"Yes, But of course the gun in his right hand says that, too."

The chief flipped the doll face up and Sarah's eyes roamed its face. "They got the hazel eyes right, too, as well as the curls." Tiny black insulated wire had been fashioned into ringlets that protruded from under the peaked cap.

"Thanks for calling this in, Sarah. I appreciate it."

Sarah realized Chief James was dismissing her. "Of course. May you get to the bottom of this soon. I wonder if an Officer Grimes doll is next." If Sarah was making a Candace doll, she'd definitely make Maple the rabbit, too. She wished whoever made her doll had put Whiskey by her side, as they were rarely apart.

"I guess we can only wait and see. Have a good day, Sarah. Bye, Whiskey." The chief ran his hand along the cattle dog's spine and Whiskey smiled at him.

Then Sarah and Whiskey walked the last few blocks to the Coiffure. After she got inside, put their breakfast on the table and the salads in the fridge, and looped her apron over her head, Sarah pulled her phone from her back pocket and showed Emily the photos she had taken while waiting for Chief James. The little doll hung from the braided threads around its neck from the nut with the small embroidery of BEAMS visible on a patch on the shirt.

"Wow, Sarah. This is incredible. I mean it looks mostly like him, as much as cloth can. Is that face made of pantyhose?"

"It might be. I wonder if the police lab has taken one apart and broken it down and catalogued its component parts. Where's the closest fabric store to here? Do you know?"

"There used to be a quilt shop here, but it closed when I was maybe ten." Emily bit into her eclair and moaned. "So good." She closed her eyes as she chewed. She was once again in all black: still black dyed hair, but in a messy bun with a pumpkin colored ribbon looped around it, a black sweatshirt over black leggings tucked into black motorcycle boots. She had even painted her short fingernails black.

"So the quilt shop closed..." Sarah prompted, taking a bite of her own eclair. *Wow, it was good.*

"Yes, the quilt shop closed. So now I think the closest fabric store might be in Cedar Rapids. Hold on." Emily pulled out her phone and did a search. "Um, there's a national chain store in a town twenty minutes away, otherwise it's a drive into the city."

Sarah started thinking aloud. "The police may or may not visit the closest fabric store to see if the maker got the fabrics and vinyl and whatever there, as this may not be a priority for them, what having a murder to solve."

Emily interrupted with, "Yes, especially since making effigies isn't a crime. Plus, that tiny gun isn't going to be found in any fabric store. Maybe the person ordered it and the fabric and everything they needed online." Emily typed something else into her phone and then she said, "Amazon even sells dollhouse size guns and so does eBay. Rifles, handguns, even miniature semi-automatic weapons."

"Oh great," Sarah mumbled. "Just what dollhouses and small children who play with them need."

"Yeah, that's kind of scary, huh? I find where the dolls are being left interesting. I'm sure it isn't random, but they are being left in plain sight where anyone could stumble across them."

"Oh, speaking of that. I didn't tell you that Bill, Janice, and Gladys ate at the restaurant next door last night and Janice spotted an effigy of Jared hanging from our outside doorknob. They called the police, and Candace brought it by so we could see it."

"Wow, Sarah. That was nice of her."

"Jared acted like he was honored to be made into an effigy and he kept raving about the design and attention to details and artistry."

Emily snickered. "I can hear him in my head. But he isn't wrong, you know. Someone is spending a lot of time making each one. What did his look like?"

Sarah pulled out her phone. Last night before they went to bed, she had Jared share the photos he took. She showed those to Emily, who ooohed and awwed over the teensy but realistic book, the coffee cup, and effigy Jared's startling green eyes that were identical to his own. "This is amazing." Emily dragged out the second a in the word for emphasis.

"So you're on team effigy now?" Sarah smirked.

"I'm always on team art, Sarah. You know that." Emily took a big gulp of coffee and then shoved the last of the eclair into her mouth. As she chewed, the door of the Coiffure flung open and Whiskey raced to warn off the intruder, until he saw that it was Annabelle, a sable coated Akita, and her human Drake Farmer, whose flawless mocha skin made Sarah envious. Sometimes she hated her freckles and moles and all of the marks that came with being a red-head.

Annabelle stood stock still, letting Whiskey sniff her all over, before she tossed her head over her shoulder at Drake, as if demanding he let her off leash so she could go off with Whiskey, Her plume of a tail wagged once, deliberate and queenly, as if she were granting him the honor of her attention. Drake chuckled at her theatrics, loosening his grip slightly on the leash, while Sarah couldn't help but notice how naturally the two dogs fell into step—like they'd been partners in mischief all along.

"Give us three hours, please," Sarah said.

"Of course," Drake turned toward the door and Sarah admired the way his muscles moved inside his cashmere sweater as he opened it and walked outside. His black 5-series BMW was parked at the curb and its passenger window displayed telltale signs of dog slobber, as Annabelle preferred to ride shotgun and hang her head from the window and enjoy the wind through her fur.

"Wouldn't he and Katie Smith be a stunning couple?" Sarah sighed.

Emily had removed Annabelle's collar and was leading both dogs toward the walk-in tub.

Whiskey parked his posterior right next to the tub door, but Emily asked him to move so she could reach the akita and start the water. He relocated six inches and leaned against Emily's right leg, letting her know he wasn't going anywhere.

At least until the door opened again...and then he was off to greet the newcomers: Rosa Torres and Tiny the toy poodle. Rosa wore a knee-length red sweater dress and black boots and always reminded Sarah of a Disney princess, with her olive skin and wavy past-her-shoulders black hair. She was in her forties but was fit with flawless skin and Sarah thought she could easily pass for her late twenties. Tiny was held in the crook of one of her arms, close to Rosa's heart.

"*Buenos dias,*" Sarah said.

"Good morning, Sarah. Hi, Emily," Rosa greeted.

"How are you and Tiny today?"

"We are good. He's a bit frightened to get a bath, as always. But I know he's in good hands with you." She kissed the top of Tiny's curly little head and murmured, "You behave for Sarah, *muchacho.*" Then she passed him into Sarah's outstretched hands.

"He'll be ready in about an hour."

"Okay. I'll go wait at Java and Juice." With that, Rosa headed out the door and walked on the sidewalk toward Main Street.

"We couldn't have much difference in size right now, Sarah."

Emily's arms were deep in the tub washing Annabelle's underside. Akitas have thick, dense undercoats with a top coat of rough, waterproof fur so they are not easy to bathe. Fortunately for members of the breed, their human companions, and the groomers, they didn't need a lot of bathing. This was Annabelle's major fall shedding, the time called "blowing the coat," which was why professional care was so important. She mostly came to see Sarah and Emily twice a year, unless she got into something nasty in between.

Sarah carried Tiny to one of the regular tubs, but before she placed the dog in the huge-for-him stainless steel basin, she put a smaller plastic turquoise blue bowl inside. She ran water until it was warm and added an inch to the bowl, then placed the dog into the bowl. Sarah cupped water into her hand and started to wet the dog. Tiny shook with nerves and his black eyes looked like two glistening beads of onyx, wide with worry, following Sarah's every move as if she were about to betray him to the deep end of the ocean instead of a shallow bath. His little body quivered, but he stayed put, trusting her hands even as his paws curled delicately against the slick plastic.

Sarah started the water through the hose at barely more than a trickle and drizzled water all over him, smoothing it into his springy gray fur. Once he was thoroughly wet, she added a dime-size dollop of shampoo and massaged it all over his body. At the calm, steady pressure of her fingers, Tiny closed his eyes and released his tension.

Sarah wished he could stay that way, in that place of peace and calm, but she knew as soon as she started the rinse water, he'd be back into panic mode. And she wasn't wrong.

Five minutes later, she had Tiny engulfed in a bath towel with only his nose peeking from between the folds. Sarah carried him to a grooming table.

Emily was still wrestling with the akita's coat and Sarah wasn't sure which of them—Annabelle or Em—were wearing more soap suds.

"I'll help you as soon as I'm done with Tiny," Sarah said. She trimmed and styled Tiny's hair then cleaned his ears and clipped his nails. And then she brushed Tiny's tiny teeth, which were like sharp, delicate rice grains lined up in a row. When she was done, Sarah gave Tiny a hug, and then set the little dog down on the floor.

Whiskey approached him slowly, like he knew any fast movements would send the dog scampering. And right before he reached the poodle, Whiskey laid down on his belly, with his feet and arms stretched and his head between them.

Tiny eyed him suspiciously, and when Whiskey didn't move, Tiny crept up to his ear and took a sniff.

Sarah smiled. Inside, she felt like a proud dog mama, grateful that Whiskey's intuition instructed him exactly how to handle his guest. She gazed at them for one more beat before scurrying over to help Emily finish Annabelle's bath.

"My finger muscles are aching from all of the working the water and shampoo in, and look at this?" Emily removed her hands from Annabelle's haunches and they were covered in clumps of white fur, soggy with suds.

"We probably should have brushed before bathing," Sarah said.

"I know." Em blew out an exasperated breath. "I forgot. I knew the bath would take forever so I wanted to get started right away.

Which was clearly the wrong move." She shrugged and then said, "Wow. I didn't realize my shoulders were so tight. Okay, dog, let's get this bath finished, for both of our sakes." Emily turned on the water and maneuvered the hose to the middle of Annabelle's back.

As the water made contact, Annabelle shook, sending sprays of soapy bombs flying in every direction, exploding on the walls, the floor, and both groomers. Emily squealed, shielding her face with her arms, while Sarah just laughed, wiping a sudsy streak from her cheek. Whiskey barked from his place on the floor with Tiny—who mimicked with a high-pitched ruff of his own—as if cheering Annabelle on, the whole scene turning into more splash zone than grooming session.

But Sarah's brain brought her laughter to a halt. Just like the water and shampoo and the act of washing triggered the reaction of the dog shaking and spraying that water and suds everywhere, high school physics class taught Sarah Newton's Third Law of Motion. The death of Paul Whitmore was an action. A violent action. *But what and where were the reactions? If they looked for those, would that help them solve the case?*

CHAPTER 15

Sarah and Emily finished rinsing Annabelle without any more drama. Then they threw two oversized bath towels over the dog. Emily took the back end and Sarah the front and they rubbed as much of the water from Annabelle's fur that they could, before Sarah led the dog to a grooming table at almost floor level. A hydraulic lift brought Annabelle to the perfect level for the rest of her spa treatment. Sarah checked the dog's ears while Emily started using the undercoat rake to pull out clumps of blown-out fur.

"So, Em, right after Annabelle's sudden bath of us, I had a bit of an epiphany. Do you remember Newton's Third Law of Motion?"

"Is that the action reaction one?"

Sarah grinned. "It most definitely is. I've been trying to learn who Paul was and why he moved to Cottageville. But his death was an action. Maybe we should be looking for a reaction. Who did his death benefit? Who is reacting to it and how?" Sarah felt proud of herself for thinking this way.

Em's eyes narrowed and her lips pursed before she said, "But, Sarah, what if his death wasn't an action. What if it was a reaction?"

"Uhh," Sarah's eyes widened. She was stunned by Emily's question and the fact that it hadn't occurred to her.

"Or, maybe Paul's death was both. Newton's Law says the action and reaction don't have to be cause and effect or sequential. They can be simultaneous."

Sarah's face squinched into confusion with a furrow so deep it could have been in a cornfield. "Wait—so you're saying Paul's death could've been setting something in motion, *and* at the same time, someone else responding to something he already did?" Her voice carried equal parts awe and frustration, as if Emily had just handed her a riddle wrapped in another riddle.

"Yes, exactly." She continued raking the akita's fur and said, "Let's walk through what we know about Paul. He was interested in Cottageville's history. He was originally born into the Buffalo family and left after high school and changed his last name."

Sarah chimed in, "He worked for one of those big consulting firms and had retired."

"Okay," Emily said. "Is that all we know? If it is, let's discuss what we know about the Buffalo family, beyond John Beams having to taser Bunky and hauling him off to jail the day his mama was buried."

Sarah had moved on to clipping Annabelle's nails. "Mayor Trish or someone said there were originally three brothers who had sort of homesteaded or bought the land and that it was more than three hundred acres. I think she said more than one hundred and fifty acres a piece. Then it was handed down to the sons, which would have been Bunky and Paul's fathers most likely. Not sure if there was another brother, too, and more cousins. And Bunky's dad died when he was young and his mom never remarried, so I guess Bunky inherited the farm."

"All of it?" Emily asked.

"I have no idea. The plat map shows the parcels and their large sizes but doesn't show ownership."

"Maybe you need to go back and see Martha and ask her to fill in some of the names for you on the plat map. She loves you so you could probably get her to do it."

"Yes, that sounds like a good idea. Oh, and Mayor Trish said Paul's dad died and she thought both he and his mom left around the same time. I forgot that part."

Whiskey lifted his head when he saw movement through the glass in the door. He nudged his tiny friend, who had fallen asleep against him. Then they both ran to greet Rosa. Annabelle turned her head and looked over her shoulder at the commotion, but she stayed on the table.

Emily had nearly finished with the rake and already had the brush in hand, ready for the next step.

Sarah said under her breath, "I've got this," and walked toward the counter to swipe Rosa's credit card. She had Tiny tucked under her arm. "He smells so fresh and clean. *Muchas gracias, señorita.* We'll see you again in six weeks."

When Rosa closed the green door, Sarah turned back to Emily and Annabelle. She took a step toward the grooming table when Emily said, "Do you know how the fathers died?"

"I don't." Sarah grabbed a brush and started at Annabelle's left shoulder.

Emily ran her brush down the dog's right side. "Who would know?"

"Maybe someone who was here back in the day."

"How old is Bunky?"

"I don't know. At least sixty, maybe sixty-five."

"So who lived in Cottageville six or seven decades ago that is still here?"

"Gladys. Mayor Trish's dad. Bill's family. I can't think of anyone else."

"Call Gladys. Or maybe invite her throuple—" Emily flashed Sarah a Cheshire cat grin—"over for dinner at your house and ask Gladys to relive the past and brainstorm with the others. Janice knows how to locate information. We clearly haven't found all of the pieces yet."

Sarah hated that they hadn't. Her agreement with the chief to focus on Paul's life instead of his death felt stymieing. She wished she had never conceded. "Let me see what Jared has planned for supper, but that definitely seems like a solid plan. Do you want to come too?"

"Nah. Hot date tonight. It's gonna be a full moon so we're

picnicking near the water tower and checking out the stars."

"Who said romance is dead?" Sarah joked. "Wear a down jacket. It's been near freezing temps at night."

"We aren't spending the night, silly. But your point is valid. I will bundle up and bring a wool blanket in case we get cold."

When they finally finished grooming Annabelle, she hopped down from the table and shook as if she needed to style her own fur. Then, with Whiskey by her side, they trotted to the front door and waited, like they wanted to go outside. Sarah put leashes on both of them and walked them outside and across the street to a grassy area so they could take care of business. As she was bringing them back into the Coiffure, Drake Farmer's beemer pulled to the curb and Annabelle wrenched Sarah's arm as she tried to get to her car.

"Whoa, girl. Don't hurt, Sarah," Drake said as he slammed the car to a stop and jumped out with the motor still running. "Let me." He reached his hand out for Annabelle's leash.

"It's okay," Sarah said. "She was a good girl through all of that work. We just finished and I took the dogs out to pee."

Drake walked Annabelle back into the Coiffure and paid Sarah and Emily in cash with a generous tip for both of them. "I know this time of year with her fur blowing out is challenging. I'm so grateful for you both and that I don't have to take care of this." He chuckled. "She looks amazing and at least five pounds lighter."

"Yes, we had a toy poodle in here at the same time, and we could have made at least three more toy poodles from Annabelle's loose fur." Emily cackled at her own comment as she swept clumps into a dustpan.

After Drake and Annabelle left, Sarah and Emily sat down to lunch, and Sarah texted Jared. "Hey, do we have plans for dinner? I'm thinking of inviting Gladys, Bill, and Janice over." And as soon as the words had flown from her brain through her fingertips and into her phone, she remembered Jared had game night. "Nevermind. I remembered you will be with the guys."

Jared sent back a smiley face followed by the blowing a kiss emoji.

Sarah started a four-way text between herself and her early octogenarian friends. They all responded that they'd love to have a meal with her. Gladys asked if Kahlo and Cassatt were invited. Janice asked what she could bring. Bill told the group he was bringing a bottle of wine.

Sarah replied, "Dogs are always welcome. A green salad? I was thinking of ordering Chinese food. Or would you prefer pizza? Of course you just ate Italian last night."

Just then Jared texted, "Hey, I'm not sure if you noticed, but I put a bunch of chicken and a sauce in the slow cooker this morning. There's plenty. Serve it over rice. I'll eat some before I go."

Sarah smiled at her phone. Jared was so great about taking care of them and making sure she ate well. It was one of the many reasons she loved him. And...she never noticed the slower cooker was on the kitchen counter this morning. The only time she had been in the kitchen had been to pour a cup of coffee to wake herself up and to give Whiskey some grain-free kibble. And for those two things, she hadn't even turned on the light.

"I love you. Thank you," she responded to Jared.

To her friends, she wrote, "New plan. Come around six. Jared made food. Janice, please bring that salad. Bill, thank you in advance for the wine. Gladys, can't wait to see the girls."

To Emily, she said, "I'm all set for tonight. I just hope Gladys remembers what happened to the Buffalo men. She may have been young at the time."

At five-thirty, Sarah said goodbye to Jared, fed Whiskey his supper, and hopped into the shower to rinse off the day's dander and dog hair. She threw on her alma mater's sweatshirt featuring the University of Washington husky with jeans and she had the table set by the time her guests arrived. Janice, Gladys, and Bill arrived together as Bill and Gladys and the poodles had walked from their houses and then picked up Janice at hers.

"Lovely night for a walk," Gladys said. "Cool, but the stars have just come out and it is clear so they are shining brightly." She wore a purple coat over a white sweater and navy pants.

Whiskey was overjoyed to see Kahlo and Cassatt. He thumped his tail and was almost bouncing waiting for them to be let off leash so they could run.

"Hang on, dog," Sarah said, bending down to help Gladys with her girls.

After taking her guests' coats and putting them in the closet, Sarah led her friends into the dining room and said she'd be right back with the food. "Janice, do you need tongs for the salad?" she yelled over her shoulder on her way into the kitchen.

"I brought some," Janice said. "Dressing, too." She was wearing a light yellow track suit with a string of pearls around her neck. This made Sarah smile. Her neighbor always exuded class like she was a royal.

"Do you need help?" Bill asked Sarah, trailing after her, in the same clothing he had worn this morning when Sarah saw him on his front porch. "I can carry something. Or give me a corkscrew and I'll open the wine."

Sarah handed Bill the corkscrew and the bowl of rice. She carried the bowl with the chicken in a chili cream sauce plus a side of steamed carrots. Jared had picked up a few Mexican chocolate bars somewhere that he gave her to offer people as dessert.

Once everyone had food on their plates, Bill raised his wine glass and offered a toast to "friendship and health." They touched glasses and smiled at each other before digging into the food. The dogs had zoomed through the house while Sarah and Bill were getting the food from the kitchen, but now they were lying on the rug in the living room, tongues hanging out, trying to catch their breaths.

After a few minutes of eating, Sarah said, "Gladys and Bill, I wondered if I could pick your brains a little about some of the town's history."

"Of course, dear. What would you like to know?" Gladys asked.

"Someone told me Bunky Buffalo's dad died when he was young. Do you remember that? And do you know how he died?"

Gladys touched her cloth napkin to her lips and her eyes widened behind her glasses. "It's been a long time since I've thought of that. It was many years ago."

"Yes, the person who told me thought maybe he was five or ten at the time. But it was before they were born."

Gladys nodded her head. "I think five may be right." She looked at Bill for confirmation.

"That sounds about right," he said.

"Was Mr. Buffalo sick?"

Gladys shook her head. "No. It was rather sudden. Farm equipment accident, I believe. Something like that. It was tragic. Left his mother all alone with the boy, scraping to get by."

Janice's shrewd eyes looked over her wine glass at Sarah. "Why the interest in Buffalo family history?"

Sarah looked from Janice to Bill to Gladys and then back to Janice. "Paul Whitmore was born Paul Buffalo. He's two years younger—or at least two grades younger—than Bunky and went to Cottageville High. I think he's Bunky's cousin."

Janice asked, "Do you think that connection has something to do with Paul showing up in town and getting himself killed?"

"I don't know," Sarah admitted. "I don't know why he left. Apparently his mom did too around the same time."

Gladys gasped. "I didn't put the two together. Paul was a towheaded boy, kind of quiet, but I always thought that was because his dad was loud and brash so he and his mother tried not to draw attention to themselves."

"Were they abused?" Janice asked.

Gladys pursed her lips and squinted, like she was deep in thought. "I don't think so. At least we never saw signs of physical harm. In a town like this one, word would have gotten around. Paul and his mother were calm, respectful. He was studious. Bunky was a more active boy. He couldn't sit still. Always wanted to know how things worked. He was good with his hands but fidgety."

"I had Paul my first year of teaching at the high school," Bill said. "I never put that boy together with the man I met a few months ago. But he was always interested in history." After getting out of the military and going to university, Bill had taught history at Cottageville High.

"Do you remember Paul and his mother leaving town?" Sarah asked. Then she ate a few more bites of chicken and rice. It was really good.

"His father had a fatal heart attack, I think it was. No one ever said anything, but I thought maybe with nothing tying them to the land with him gone, that that's why they left. Farming was never going to be Paul's occupation," Gladys said.

Janice asked, "Do you know, Glad, if Paul or his mother ever returned to Cottageville?"

"Not that I had heard or seen. Until Sarah said Paul Buffalo and Paul Whitmore were the same person, I never would have known. It's been four decades or more since anyone has mentioned them."

Bill took a sip of wine and then said, "I wonder what brought him back to town, and why he was secretive about who he was. When he talked to me on my porch a few times, he asked a lot of questions but never said he had grown up here or that I had him in class. He acted like he knew very little about Cottageville." Bill frowned then mumbled, "I liked the guy enough...but now I'm not so sure."

Sarah flashed Bill a weak smile. "Do you feel lied to or betrayed?"

"Those may be stronger words, but I definitely feel something, like he wasn't being honest. Which makes me question why?" Bill's eyes were back on his food, and he stabbed a carrot with his fork.

Janice asked, "What have you uncovered about his life beyond that?"

Sarah ran through the list of things that she and Emily had reviewed earlier in the day. She ended with, "He doesn't have much of an online presence. Katie Smith told me a few states he lived in previously that she pulled from his background check. But it didn't add up to much. We could find no children, spouse, or any relatives connected with his Whitmore name. And only the old yearbook online showed him as a Buffalo."

"He was really interested in the history of the town," Bill said.

"Yes," Sarah said. "I have a lot of the books he had checked out from the library in my living room. I've been going through them. Carole was so nice to look at his borrowing history and she had talked to him maybe more than most of the other people in town, since he was in the library doing research often in his short time here."

"Do we know what he was looking for in that history?" Gladys asked.

"Not exactly," Sarah finished the food on her plate and after she swallowed, she added, "He never told Carole what he was looking for beyond a specific photo and information about the town. Though I had wondered if it was something about the land. I got a plat map from Martha but I really need to go back to her and find out who owns some of the parcels."

Bill said, "Speaking of land and parcels, that developer is at it again trying to force people to sell their land."

"Are you talking about the one who wants to buy a couple or few hundred acres for a subdivision and whatnot?" Sarah asked.

"Yes, that's the one," Bill said. "Every five years or so one comes a-knocking. This one may be one of the worst. They call themselves Heartland Homesteads but the name is a misnomer. More like homestead marauders. The owner loves to build new shiny things without any care on the environmental impact or the way of life of the people already living in the area. Bigger and more doesn't mean better."

"Where exactly does he want to build? I heard it was off the interstate."

"Yes, somewhere off there," Gladys said. "I dread the traffic that will create."

Janice drank the last of the wine in her glass. "It would bring a lot of change. This was a really good wine, Bill. Thank you. And Sarah, what a delicious dinner. Give our compliments to your chef." Her eyes twinkled with the last comment. "So, how can we help you solve this mystery? And what about those effigies? Someone said you found another one today?"

"I did, an Officer Beams doll, though in some ways that feels like a long time ago. It's been a long day. Chief James and I aren't sure the effigies are a warning or threat. Jared saw his doll as a huge compliment and he was awed by the artist's attention to detail and accuracy. As to how you can help me with the Paul Whitmore killing, can you think of what reason he'd come back to town and keep his identity a secret?"

Gladys said, "And we don't know why he changed his name in the first place. Do we know when?"

"I don't."

Janice reached toward Sarah and patted her hand. "I will find that."

Sarah had no doubt she would. Sarah asked if anyone wanted a cup of tea or decaf coffee and some dessert. She excused herself for a minute to look in on the dogs and to grab the chocolate from the kitchen. As she was walking back into the dining room, a thought occurred to her.

"Hey, Gladys or Bill," she said as she put the chocolate bars on the table, "do you remember if Paul had any sisters or brothers?"

"Not that I recall. But then again, they did keep to themselves."

Bill said, "I only had Paul in school. Bunky had already graduated and I had no more Buffalos."

Janice volunteered, "I'll check the birth records, too, to be sure."

Bill suggested, "Let's have dinner again tomorrow night at my place. Sarah, bring Jared and Whiskey. If we all put our heads together, maybe we can get to the bottom of this."

Sarah wasn't sure if they needed more minds or more clues. But she agreed to be there at six and to bring an autumn salad.

CHAPTER 16

The next evening after a busy day of grooming that provided little time for sleuthing, Sarah arrived home to find Jared mixing roasted pumpkin and pumpkin seeds with baby kale, slivers of purple cabbage, strips of red bell pepper, and half-moons of celery in a big bowl. A maple, ginger, thyme olive oil and white vinegar based dressing was in a small to-go container.

"Wow. That looks amazing. A rainbow in a bowl, and it smells like the perfume of pumpkin patches and cinnamon-laced cider."

"Yes, without the hay overlay." Jared smiled and kissed the tip of her nose. "I'll feed Whiskey while you shower and then we need to go."

"I know. I know. Onyx's humans were late picking him up and Emily had a class to get to so Whiskey and I had to wait."

"Is Onyx that huge black Russian dog?"

"Yes, he's a terrier. Sweet guy. But his female human is a bit overwhelmed. She has five elementary school aged kids, and she had to pick them up from their various activities before she picked up Onyx."

"Five?" Jared's eyes bugged from his skull like a cartoon character, or at least that's what his widened eyes reminded Sarah of. She saw shock and fear and that caused her to chuckle.

"Yeah. One kid in each grade. I don't think the parents are fans of birth control." Sarah giggled. "Though they did have Onyx neutered."

"Sounds like they don't need a litter of puppies on top of their human litter." Jared smiled.

"Nope," Sarah called over her shoulder on her way through the living room to their bedroom. She took a two-minute shower, put on a clean royal blue cashmere sweater with jeans, put her arms into a down vest and zipped it up, and slid her feet into fleece-lined boots and was ready to go. Jared and Whiskey were waiting at the front door with the salad.

"Do we need to bring anything else?" Sarah asked.

"There's a bottle of sparkling wine on the counter, if you want to grab that."

They stopped at Janice's house just as she was coming out the door in a long black, buttoned-up coat and black rubber bottomed boots. "Aren't your arms cold, Sarah?" Janice asked.

"No. The sweater is warm enough. How are you today, Mrs. Jenkins?"

"Fine. Just fine. I can't wait to share the information I have collected. But that will have to wait until we are all at Bill's. Jared, how is everything in the book publishing world? Are you still touring?"

As Whiskey led the way up the hill toward the park, Jared filled them in on his latest opportunities to be a podcast guest, to give a lecture, and the latest translation rights that had been sold. He ended the update with, "My agent said one of the streaming services has asked for a meeting about creating a movie or a show based on my characters."

"What!?" Sarah exclaimed. "You didn't tell me."

Jared grinned. "I did right now. Besides, it was just a request. Nothing has been scheduled. I don't know any details. I don't even know if I'll do it or if they will want to."

"It's still a big deal for them to even reach out," Sarah insisted.

"I agree with Sarah on this," Janice said. "If they reached out, that means you're on Hollywood's radar, and while it may be only a blip, you have to explore the possibility."

"Do you ever think you'd like to share your life more publicly, Mrs. Jenkins?" Jared asked. "It's been extraordinary."

"It has. But it has also been filled with secrets that are better off going to the grave with me. Too many people could be unfairly affected otherwise, as well as systems and, um, security." Janice's eyes trailed to the ground in front of them as they walked.

Sarah and Jared knew their elderly neighbor still occasionally was hired by governments, museums, banks, and other organizations for the expertise she developed after working decades for some of the world's best known agencies.

They crossed the street into the park, following the winding path, with Whiskey as usual darting back and forth as he trailed after invisible scents. As they neared the big evergreen, Whiskey beelined for the tree and raised his nose in the air, audibly sniffing. He let loose a single, sharp bark.

"What is it, boy?" Sarah asked, leaving the trail to go to the tree. Her eyes went from Whiskey's face to where his eyes seemed to be fixated on the branches. Sarah expected to see a possum or a cat, with the way Whiskey was behaving. Instead, hanging on a branch one above her eye level was an ambulance made out of cloth and stuffed, with two dolls popping out the side windows, both with black hair and in medic coveralls, one clearly male and one female.

Sarah turned on her phone's flashlight to get a better look, as Jared and Mrs.Jenkins flanked her sides. "I'll call the chief," Janice said.

"It's so different from the others," Jared said, "since it has the ambulance. The Parks are almost secondary."

"Yes. And the nooselike braided loop is attached in a way that makes this look like a Christmas ornament." The loop had been stitched to the center of the roof."

Janice disconnected the call. "Officer Grimes is on her way. I'll text Bill and Glad to let them know we will be a few minutes late."

"Thank you," Sarah said. "I wonder why the focal point of this effigy is the ambulance and not the people."

"The people are there," Jared said, turning his head at it one way and then the other as if he wanted to capture all of the perspectives. "But they aren't done as realistically. I mean, I've never seen the Parks waist deep hanging out their windows with their arms in the air. Chief James and John were in their uniforms. You were in your Halloween costume which was a riff on a big part of your identity. Mine included my life as author and artist as well as my role at Java and Juice."

"This is the Parks' role in the community," Janice said.

"It is. But the way they are positioned reminds me of people in a rollercoaster who throw their hands up right before they go down a big hill."

"Maybe the maker is trying to capture that excitement of the Parks in the way they serve their neighbors," Sarah said.

"But I've never seen them joyous to be called out to save someone's life. They are solemn and respectful and professional."

"They are." Janice's voice was steady and knowing as she said, "But it is a bit of a rush to help people out of their crises and to help them get a second chance at life. Maybe this was the artist's way to capture that inner happiness and satisfaction at making such a difference."

Candace Grimes came jogging up the path and then she hustled over to the tree. "You. Again," she said to Sarah.

Sarah grinned at her friend. "It was Whiskey. He found it and alerted us."

"Of course he did," Officer Grimes said. "He's a highly intelligent boy. Aren't you, Whiskey? You're such a good boy." She scratched her fingers all around his neck and head and he leaned into it.

Then she stopped, took a bunch of photos with her phone, donned gloves from the pocket of her jacket, and removed the ambulance from the tree, placing it into an evidence bag. As she did the last part, she mumbled, "I wish we knew what these were evidence of."

"That's what I was just thinking." Sarah laughed. "Literally word for word."

Janice cleared her throat before saying, "Have you considered it maybe guerilla art?"

"That's what I wondered," Jared admitted.

"What's guerilla art?" Candace asked. "You mean like graffiti and things?"

"That's one type of guerilla art," Janice said. "But I was thinking more like AnonyMouse."

"Ooo, cool. I love that," Jared interjected.

"What's an AnonyMouse?" Sarah asked.

Jared eyed Mrs. Jenkins like he wanted to see who was going to answer. He nodded his head once toward her encouraging her to go on.

"AnonyMouse is in Europe. It's a collective of artists, as far as we know, that creates fairytale-like buildings in cities across the continent and they are meant to be discovered as surprises, kind of like these effigies or whatever they are."

"So no one knows who is making them?" Sarah asked.

"No. Or at least no one who is a part of it is coming forward. The whole point is it is about the art itself and not the artist," Mrs. Jenkins explained.

Officer Grimes asked, "Do you think that is what is going on here?"

"I have no idea, but it is a possibility we can't rule out."

"Thank you for calling this in," Candace said.

"Doing my civic duty." Mrs Jenkins patted Officer Grimes twice on her forearm, before Whiskey led them all up the path toward Bill's house.

A half an hour later, when Whiskey and the poodles were curled up on the living room carpet, and all of the humans were gathered around Bill's dining table with bowls of pasta and salad, Bill raised his glass of wine and said, "I'm calling this an early Thanksgiving since I'm so grateful to my friends of all ages with two feet or four."

Sarah smiled that the dogs were included, and her heart felt aglow from the love of the people in that room. They were her chosen, local family.

Partway through the meal, Janice announced, "Whitmore was Paul's mother's maiden name. She changed it back to that immediately after her husband died and had Paul do the same."

"In this state," Jared asked, "do you have to include a reason for your name change? I know in some states you do."

"You do," Janice said, "but it can be rather vague, such as 'this name better suits me' or 'i like this name better.' Paul's mother wrote 'returning to maiden name after husband's death'."

"What did Paul's name change form say?" Sarah asked.

"'Father died, taking same name as mother',"

"So we don't really know why," Gladys said.

"No. But as part of the name change process, you have to list any property you own. And here's where it gets interesting. The about-to-be Mrs. Whitmore claimed to own no property, but Paul Buffalo had provided proof of owning two hundred and fifty-eight acres of farmland."

"What?!" Sarah exclaimed. "The land bypassed the wife for the son?"

Mrs. Jenkins nodded her head. "I dug around a little. The way the original three Buffalo brothers set up their wills was that their oldest sons did the inheriting of the land."

"And Bunky and Paul were the only heirs. Not just the only male heirs," Bill concluded.

Janice took a sip of wine and then said, "There are two birth records for female Buffalos. One a year older than Paul, one a year younger." She paused and looked from person to person around the table. "But there are no death records, or school records, or records of any kind beyond the issuance of the birth certificates." Her pale lips were in a grim line.

Sarah started to ask, "How does one—" at the same time Bill asked, "So they just disappeared?"

"Looks that way," Janice said. "Might be buried on that land."

Silence filled the air and no one moved, letting Janice's words sink deep into their hearts, minds, and souls.

Sarah broke the silence with these words, spoken just above a whisper: "Paul must have known."

Gladys' eyes were watery. She wiped one bent with arthritis finger under the right one, before she said, "The property holds a lot of sorrow. No wonder Paul and his mother left as soon as they could."

"But why would he come back?" Jared asked.

"Maybe it has to do with that proposed development," Bill said. "While you two were at work and while Janice was shaking government trees, I visited the county clerk's office to see if Martha knew anything about Heartland Homesteads. Turns out their CEO has been pressuring the county too, talking a good game about how development would be good for the county. He cites the jobs he'd be hiring for locally, the tax revenue it would generate, and he's promised road improvements and to help build a new school."

"Did you find out exactly where he wants to do this?" Sarah asked, starting to feel hope that they may just make sense of Paul's murder yet.

"Yes. Some of it is county woodlands. The rest is owned by—and you may have guessed this—a trust. The Buffalo Brothers Trust to be exact."

CHAPTER 17

Sarah gasped and dropped her fork. "Do you think the developer killed Paul?" Her eyebrows were in her hairline.

"I don't know," Bill said. "Neither do you. It could be a coincidence."

Janice interrupted, "In my line of work those are rare."

Bill nodded. "The thing is, we don't know who is officially a part of the trust or what the trust says. Other than Janice telling us the land has been handed down through the male heirs, we don't know if it is still that way. Bunky has no children that we know of, and you said last night you found no family for Paul." He looked at Janice to see if she had confirmed that.

Janice said, "That's what the official records look like, too."

Gladys said, "What we need to do is to talk to Bunky. Maybe he knows what happened to Paul and why."

Very quietly, Janice said, "He may because he may have killed him."

Gladys jumped to his defense. "I can't see the Bunky I know doing something like this. I've never seen him with a temper, even as a child. He was hyper, sure. But never angry. He's always had a well of deep sadness inside him and sometimes it overflows."

"You mean like the night of his mama's death when he was shooting up things on the farm?" Sarah asked.

"Exactly. That wasn't rage. That was despair. It broke my heart," Gladys said.

Jared asked, "I don't know a lot about trusts. Is there any way to find out what one says?"

"Not really," Janice explained. "The trust is mostly between the lawyer or lawyers who drafted it and the family members involved. You may see public notices mentioning a trust, like when real estate is bought or sold that is held in one. Or sometimes when I've done an asset deep dive on a target or person of interest, you'll see companies and businesses and cars and homes and yachts and all kinds of things held by a trust or even a trust inside a trust. Some people try to be clever." Janice shook her head back and forth with a scowl on her face like she was disgusted.

"I wonder what happens if Paul and Bunky are the principals of the trust and there are no successors." Sarah reached for her phone to Google an answer.

But Janice said, "The court then will appoint a trustee. And if no legal heirs can be found, then the state takes over the land or property and will determine what happens to it."

"So if we suppose Bunky and Paul are the trustees and the end of the family lines, and they both die and there are no distant relatives, then the state takes over their property and could sell it to the developer?" Jared asked.

"After it goes through probate, yes, that could happen," Janice said.

"Do you think Bunky's life is at risk?" Sarah asked. Her brows were knit together and she vibrated with energy like she wanted to pop up from her chair and race to the Buffalo farm to foil a potential murder.

"It's a possibility. But like I said, we don't know if Bunky killed his cousin," Janice reminded.

"And we also have no proof he didn't." Sarah twisted the cloth napkin on her lap. "Could this be why the chief wanted me to focus on Paul's life? Do you think he knew all about these connections and possibilities?"

Jared reached his hand the foot distance between them and clasped her twitchy fingers. "He was clear that he didn't want you to get killed, Sarah. I don't either. No one at this table does. And right now, though we have more information, we still aren't sure what we are dealing with."

Sarah took a deep breath and audibly exhaled. Then she said, "Okay, let's review what we know. One, Paul was born a Buffalo and is from here and his mom gave birth to at least three children, two of which were girls who may not have lived very long. Two, Paul and Bunky are cousins, but when Paul's dad died, he and his mom left Cottageville and changed their last names to her maiden name. Three, a developer is trying his best to acquire the Buffalo land plus some state land." Sarah paused and looked at Bill.

"Did Martha's gossip include if the state or county was willing to sell?"

"She didn't say. Only that the developer had taken the county commissioners golfing and fishing and was laying on the 'schmoozing thicker than icing on a wedding cake,' I believe were her exact words."

Everyone at the table laughed at that descriptive turn of phrase.

"Okay, the fourth thing we know is that someone killed Paul. Most likely he was drugged and then hanged and dressed up in that scarecrow costume." Sarah shuddered.

"Which was a very public statement," Janice added. "So I believe the killer was sending a message to someone by where and the way Paul was displayed."

"Which brings us to the part we don't know," Jared said. "Was the message meant for Bunky or was Bunky sending a message to the developer? Or I guess, it could have been neither of them doing the killing nor sending the messages and unrelated to the potential development deal." He finished the wine in his glass.

"But that doesn't seem as likely," Gladys said.

"True," Janice said, "but we cannot rule out any possibilities until we are sure we have all of the facts."

Sarah said, "I want to talk to Bunky. Gladys and Bill, since he's known you two a lot of your lives, will you come with me?"

"Of course we will, Sarah," Bill said. "When would you like to go? And do you want to call ahead or show up unannounced?"

"Let me think about that. I don't really want to go out there at night. Jared and I had talked about going Friday after work, but I don't think that's a good idea now that we have more information. Do you think we could go Saturday afternoon or on Sunday? What day is best for you both?"

"Either is good for me," Gladys said.

"Me, too," Bill said. He stood and started to pick up the empty dishes on the table, stacking the bowls one inside the other.

"I'm going to do some more digging around," Janice said. "Maybe I can find an heir or uncover what Paul was searching for in all of that Cottageville history. Sarah, do you still have those library books?"

"Yes, I do. When we get back I can get them for you."

"Thank you."

A half an hour later, Sarah had passed along the books to Mrs. Jenkins, who promised to return them to her in twenty-four hours. She and Jared were getting ready for bed when she said, "The daughters are haunting me. What do you think happened to Paul's two sisters?"

"They could have been casualties of SIDS."

"But if a baby dies suddenly, wouldn't you call nine-one-one and report it?"

Jared put his arm around her and pulled Sarah toward him. "Yes, I would. But sixty years ago or more, things in this rural community may have been different. People were buried on their own property sometimes. And there may not have been an ambulance system. In fact, I don't think there was even a national nine-one-one system until Clinton was president."

"Really?" Sarah asked, absorbing comfort from Jared's heart beating against her own. They were now snuggled together, sitting up against the headboard. "You could Google it, but I'm pretty sure. So if a baby died in the fifties or sixties, maybe there wasn't anyone to call. You just dealt with it."

"That's sad," Sarah said.

Whiskey must have sensed her mood shift, because he crawled from the bottom of the bed to her and rested his chin on her leg.

"Such a sweet boy," Sarah said, absently stroking the fur between his ears.

"Thank you," Jared joked, before opening his mouth in a wide yawn. "That salad turned out exceptional. We'll have to make it again. Are you doing okay, Sarah? If you aren't, I'll stay up with you..." His voice trailed off and she knew how exhausted he was and that his alarm would be blaring in just a few hours.

"I'm good. Thank you for making that incredible salad. I love you. Let's go to sleep." Sarah lifted her chin so her lips could reach his. Then she turned out the light on her nightstand before sliding down under the covers. Whiskey's chin ended up on her chest, and he sighed and wriggled closer to her before shutting his eyes in sleep.

The next morning, Jared's alarm jarred Sarah awake. She had been in the middle of a dream where she was digging hole after hole in a field, looking for something she had buried long ago and its location couldn't be recalled. Shovel after shovel of grass and dirt moved from left to right over and over and then when Sarah saw she had uncovered nothing, she shoveled the organic matter back again from right to left until the ground was flat again. Then she moved to the next area and repeated until her arms ached and her mouth was parched and futility and loss took up residence in her chest cavity like unwelcome tenants—heavy, unmoving, and impossible to evict, pressing against her ribs with every breath as if to remind her that what she sought was gone for good, or maybe had never existed at all.

When her eyes popped open, her breathing was labored and the weight of the dream felt real. Jared was leaning over her stroking her arm. "Are you okay? You screamed but I couldn't make out any words."

Whiskey stood on all fours next to her, his chocolate eyes filled with worry, his head tilted just so, as if he could shoulder her unease himself if only she'd let him. His ears flicked forward, waiting for her to speak, and his tail gave the faintest wag—a quiet reminder that she wasn't in this alone.

"It was all so real. I was digging and digging and digging, but never found what I was looking for."

"Cue U2 song." Jared grinned and leaned down to press his lips to hers. "Are you going to be okay? I need to jump in the shower."

"I'm fine. It was only a dream." She curled onto her side and Whiskey settled with his spine against hers. They tried to go back to sleep, but only Whiskey succeeded. Sarah lay perfectly still and counted her breaths. Five counts inhale, five counts hold, five counts on the exhale. It calmed her but did not usher her back to dreamland.

When Jared had completed his morning routine and went into the kitchen for his first cup of coffee, Sarah followed him. He poured some of the black hot liquid into her mug that featured Whiskey's mug and his name and slid it across the counter to her, where she had perched on a bar stool.

"Can't go back to sleep?"

"My brain is churning like a washing machine stuck on the spin cycle—round and round, noisy, and not getting me anywhere cleaner... or clearer. It's frustrating."

Jared patted her hand. "I understand. But I'm sure you'll figure it out. You always do."

Sarah flashed him a weak smile, like she appreciated his support but currently lacked the confidence in his conviction that she'd get this. She took another sip of coffee before kissing him goodbye and telling him to have a good morning. "Give Ginger my love. We really need a girls' day. It's been too long since she and I hung out."

"I agree," Jared said. "Love you. Bye."

Whiskey raced from the bedroom to the front door to say goodbye, too. Jared bent down and hugged the dog around his neck. "You be a good boy today and take care of Sarah."

Sarah heard the deadbolt engage as Jared locked the door behind himself. She debated going back to bed at least to rest if not to sleep. But then she heard her phone chime from the bedroom. She padded in her bare feet into the room and grabbed it from the nightstand. It was a text from Mrs. Jenkins. "I see your lights are on. Are you up?"

Sarah chuckled to herself and replied, "I am. What's up?"

"I"m coming over."

"I'll pour you a cup of coffee. You take it black, right?"

"I'd rather have tea. Black with a splash of milk."

Sarah chuckled again to herself.

"Coming right up."

Sarah returned to the kitchen and put the kettle on. She pulled down a tin of English Breakfast tea and took half and half from the refrigerator. "We're getting company, Whisk," Sarah said, before letting him out the back door to do his business.

Just as he was walking into the house, Whiskey and Sarah heard a soft knock on the front door and Whiskey barked and raced so fast on the hardwoods that he lost his footing and slid into the door with a thud. Once he stood up and shook himself, he stepped back enough for Sarah to open the door. Mrs. Jenkins carried three of the library books and was wearing a quilted housecoat in a pale blue over flannel pajamas with a ruffle at the neckline. Her face was make-up free and Sarah was struck by her beauty.

"Come in, please."

The teapot whistled from the kitchen and Sarah scurried that way to stop the noise. She knew Mrs. Jenkins would follow her. She poured the water over the tea bag and pushed it, with a small bowl and spoon for after the tea had steeped, along with the half and half toward Mrs. Jenkins who had parked herself on a barstool with a back.

"Did you sleep at all?" Sarah asked.

"A couple of hours. But you know me, when the mind gets to working and a mystery needs to be solved..." Her voice faded.

"Did you come up with any answers," Sarah paused and took a sip of coffee. Then she added, "Or more questions?"

"Maybe a bit of both." Mrs. Jenkins removed the tea bag and then whitened her tea with just a drop before stirring.

"What was most likely the cause of deaths of the two daughters has been bothering me," Sarah admitted.

"Yes, but I think there's another person we forgot, one who like those daughters there is a record of, but then is forgotten."

Sarah's eyes narrowed and her brows squished together like she was going for a Frida Kahlo look while she wracked her brain trying to think of all of the players. She drew a blank.

Mrs. Jenkins smiled at her like she was proud Sarah was trying to figure it out on her own. She sipped her tea and stayed silent for a few moments until Sarah said, "I give up."

"You said yourself, three Buffalo brothers homesteaded the land. Their names, by the way, were Bernard, Milo, and Theodore. Theodore is Paul's grandfather. Bernard was the father of Bernard the second, who was the father of Bernard the third, or the guy you all call Bunky. Milo had a son also called Milo, but..." Janice paused and drank more tea.

"I've seen no Milo other than the founder in the history books," Sarah said.

"That's the thing. The records on Milo the second's life end. That's what I've been awake investigating. He doesn't get married. He doesn't have children. He doesn't even pay taxes after the age of twenty-four. It's like he ceases to exist."

"But how?" Sarah asked.

"That, my dear, is exactly what we need to find out." Mrs. Jenkins gave Sarah a sly grin, the kind that made her wrinkles fold into a map of secrets. "In small towns like ours, people don't just vanish without reason. Either he left behind something worth hiding... or someone made sure his trail went cold." She set her teacup down with a soft clink. "And I've got a hunch which it is."

CHAPTER 18

Sarah leaned forward, her mug forgotten in her hands. "Do you think he was killed? Like Paul?"

Mrs. Jenkins's eyes flickered toward the window, as though someone might be listening from the shadows beyond the glass. "If Milo the second was killed, maybe it was because whatever he knew was dangerous enough for someone to erase him entirely."

Whiskey let out a low whine and pressed his nose to Sarah's leg, as if echoing the unease that thickened the air.

"But why would no one talk about it? Not even in whispers?" Sarah asked. "Gossip is the fuel that runs through this town."

"That's what has me curious." Mrs. Jenkins drummed her

fingers on the countertop. "When a whole town goes quiet about a person, it usually means one of two things: shame...or fear. Especially when he's a son of the sort-of founding fathers of the town."

Sarah felt the dream return to her chest—the endless digging, the searching for something she couldn't find. Only now, Milo's name filled the empty hole in her mind.

"What if," she whispered, "what if Milo's disappearance is tied to Paul's death? What if someone's been keeping the same secret for generations, and Paul knew it?"

Mrs. Jenkins nodded slowly. "That's my hunch exactly. And if we don't uncover what that secret is..." She trailed off, eyes fixed on Sarah's.

"...then Bunky might be in danger," Sarah finished for her. "Would you like another cup of tea?"

"No, thank you. I should let you get ready for work. I'll keep poking around to see what I uncover. There has to be answers somewhere, official, unofficial, secrets don't stay buried forever." Mrs. Jenkins left the three library books she brought with her on Sarah's counter.

Whiskey and Sarah accompanied her to the door, with Sarah giving her a good-bye hug. "Thank you for helping with this and for using the sources you have. I appreciate you lending your expertise."

Mrs. Jenkins' smiled. "Any time, Sarah. I enjoy a good puzzle."

Sarah toasted a slice of whole grain bread and topped it with avocado. She ate standing at the counter, paging through the books Mrs. Jenkins had returned. One short tome called *Founding of Cottageville* contained a black and white photo of Milo with a pitchfork, Theodore with a scythe, and Bernard with a shotgun, with hats on their heads and overalls covering their cotton, button down shirts—according to the caption underneath—all standing in front of a round bale of hay nearly as tall as they were. The photo had been taken at a distance and was grainy so Sarah couldn't make out the expression on the men's faces but none of the three looked very old, maybe her age or younger.

When Sarah had finished her food, she showered and dressed for the day and then took Whiskey for his morning walk. She left her to-go mug at the house because it was still early and she planned to come home again before leaving for the Coiffure. Sarah followed Whiskey up their street, where she heard through his open window, her neighbor Robert Wise singing "Bohemian Rhapsody" loudly in his shower. She snickered to herself, but admired his willingness to put his everything into a song.

At the top of the hill, there was no traffic, so Sarah and Whiskey crossed the street into the park, but not before Sarah eyed the street sign to check for another effigy. She realized she was holding her breath when she saw nothing but the steel post that held the sign.

The park path was sprinkled with fallen leaves that crunched under her fleece-lined boots and released sharp, earthy perfume, like the forest exhaling one last breath before winter's silence. And that was what Sarah felt in the park during this early morning forage: silence. No scurrying of critters or chattering of squirrels that sounded like sputtering engines coming to life that drove Whiskey crazy. The air felt still; the quiet wrapped Sarah like one of Gigi's crocheted afghans. And in that atmosphere, she was confident she would solve the mystery of who murdered Paul and why.

As Whiskey and Sarah curved around the path that passed the children's playground, Sarah saw a familiar shape dangling between the steps leading to the top of the slide. "Whiskey, come," she commanded as she walked toward the playground equipment.

What was hanging before her was an Officer Candace Grimes effigy, in full uniform with hat and boots and her name embroidered on the chest patch. A small firearm seemed to be in its holster, and from what Sarah could see, all of the items on the officer's real police belt had been included on the doll. This effigy, like the other police ones, had a braided noose around its neck attaching it to the rung of the ladder.

Instead of calling the chief, Sarah sent a group text to him, John, and Candace as she wasn't sure who was currently on duty. Included in the text was a photo of the effigy.

"Not again," the chief wrote.

"Be there in five," texted Officer Beams.

"Do I really look like that?" quipped Officer Grimes.

Sarah chuckled aloud. "You're better looking and you know it," she wrote back. The effigy-Grimes' face looked made from pantyhose with threads pulled tight in a circle to create a bulbous nose, as opposed to the more angular nose on Candace's face. The doll's eyes had brown irises like her human and her lips were painted red peaks over a crimson slash of a single parenthesis turned on its side.

True to his word, John strolled down the park path five minutes later, his black hair curling around his cap, his hazel eyes sparkling in what looked to Sarah like amusement. Whiskey ran toward him with his tail swishing like a feather duster in frantic hands.

"Whiskey, my man," Officer Beams crouched and let the dog run into his open arms. He hugged Whiskey and then stood and approached Sarah and the slide. "Sarah." He nodded his head once. "This investigation looks all downhill from here."

"Very funny…or very punny, I mean. How are you today, John?"

"Just started my shift and you're my first call."

"I don't feel honored about that." Sarah smirked.

"At least it wasn't a body."

"True. I wonder if the maker will create miniatures of everyone in Cottageville, if given enough time, or if we are chosen ones for some reason."

Officer Beams picked up the Grimes effigy with his gloved hands and flipped it over to inspect the back of it. "Same precise stitching and attention to details."

"Now you sound like Jared."

Beams grinned. "As to if we'll discover these for everyone, I don't know. What I do know is I'm not a fan of the nooses around my, Grimes' and the chief's necks." He pulled at the collar of his shirt as if it was strangling him.

"I wondered what kind of statement was being made with those. Does the artist want to hang the police? Or maybe it's a pro-police statement like you aren't being given enough rope or something." Sarah frowned. "I guess it could be just as easily interpreted that you're being led around by criminals like a donkey on a rope or a horse on a lead or something."

"Did you just call me and my colleagues asses?" Beams' dimple showed in his right cheek.

"Wow, you are on a roll this morning."

"I butter hop to it and get this into the lab." Beams' grin at his own pun stretched ear to ear, and he gave a little chuckle at his own cleverness.

Sarah groaned, shaking her head, but the corner of her mouth betrayed her with the start of a smile. "You're incorrigible."

"Incorrigibly *toast-worthy*," he corrected, wagging his black eyebrows before trotting off with the evidence bag.

Whiskey started to follow him, but Sarah called him back to her. "We're going home, Whisk. I need to grab my cup and my computer and then we'll come back this way and visit Bill."

Whiskey cocked his head to the left and his right ear twitched like he was listening intently. And then he almost pranced down the path back the way they had come. Sarah quickened her steps to keep up.

Twenty minutes later, they were back in the park and just about to exit onto the sidewalk by Bill's house when Sarah saw Bunky Buffalo in his old, rusty green pick-up truck driving south on Main Street. His eyes stared straight ahead so Sarah wasn't sure he saw them, but she waved anyway. Whiskey climbed Bill's stairs and plonked his butt on the wooden porch and gave a single thump of his tail.

Bill laughed. "Give me your paw,"

Whiskey held up his right paw and waited for Bill to shake it. Before Whiskey returned his paw to the porch, Bill had fed him a beef biscuit. Whiskey raised his paw again for another shake, trying to get a second one.

"Whiskey, don't be pushy," Sarah said. "You've had one."

Whiskey's brown eyes widened and he lowered his snout as if saying, "Pleeeeaaase."

Bill chuckled and handed him another treat. "He knows how to work it, Sarah. He's very smart."

"I don't want him to act entitled," she muttered. "Whiskey and I found another effigy this morning on our early walk."

"You did, did you? Who this time?" Bill took a sip from the coffee cup that sat next to his *Courier.* He wore a quilted flannel shirt with his jeans this morning and his leather house slippers.

"Candace Grimes. In uniform."

"Is that most of the force, then?"

"The major players. No dolls of dispatch or the couple patrol cops."

"Plus the Parks and you and Jared."

"Yes. I had tea with Janice this morning. We both had problems sleeping." Sarah filled him in on Bunky's uncles' names and that one of them had disappeared. "Do you remember any rumors from when you were young about him? His name was Milo."

Bill rubbed his chin and narrowed his eyes and Sarah waited for him to think about it. "I remember that he wasn't here anymore. There was gossip that he was bootlegging and something bad happened related to that. Or I think other people accused him of going to speakeasies and running off with a showgirl or something. None of it made much sense. But I only heard the rumors as I was growing up."

"Janice and I were wondering if his disappearance had anything to do with Paul's death."

"I don't know," Bill said. Then he gave Sarah a slight smile and said, "But I'm sure you'll find out."

"I'm going to try to. Thanks for the conversation and the treats. We need to be on our way."

Bill gave Sarah a hug and patted Whiskey's spine and said he'd catch them later.

A few minutes later Sarah opened the door to Java and Juice and was surprised to see her BFF behind the register. No customers were lined up at the counter so Sarah waved to a few of her acquaintances who were seated at tables and trailed Whiskey to greet Ginger.

"Hey, bestie, I've missed you," Ginger said. She stood on her tiptoes and leaned over the counter to give Sarah a hug. Then she took Sarah's to-go cup and turned toward the coffee maker.

"I've missed you, too. I told Jared to tell you I need some girl time. When are you free?"

Ginger handed Sarah back her cup. "Sunday after Jared and I take the donuts to the Presbyterian church for their social. Or the following Sunday, any time. What are you doing for Thanksgiving?"

"Having a quiet one, I think. Are you and Daniel with both sets of parents?"

Ginger nodded. "We are hosting this year. You're welcome to come."

"Nah. I think we may ask Bill, Gladys, and Janice to come over or find other people with no place to go."

"That's sweet." Ginger bagged up two spiced muffins stuffed with apples and cream cheese and added two Thai-inspired chicken and papaya salads with sides of ginger-tahini dressing for Sarah and

Em's lunch. She rang it all up and Sarah was paying just as Jared came through the swinging doors to the kitchen carrying two baking sheets of pastries.

"Hey, love," he said.

Whiskey grinned at seeing Jared and he wagged his tail faster than gossip spread in Cottageville.

"Hey, Whiskey. Are you being a good boy?"

At the question Whiskey gave a quick yip for yes.

"I've got it," Ginger said, tossing Whiskey, a chicken biscuit. Then she lowered her voice and asked Sarah, "Have you figured out yet who killed Paul Whitmore?"

"I'm working on it," Sarah said. "I feel like it is only a matter of connecting the right dots—like the picture's already drawn, but I'm still staring at the lines instead of seeing the face."

"I'm sure you'll understand the details very soon," Ginger said.

Sarah said goodbye to her two favorite people, Ginger and Jared, and then she and Whiskey walked the rest of the way to the Coiffure, only to find Bunky Buffalo's truck parked at the curb right outside the door.

CHAPTER 19

The truck looked empty or at least no one was sitting upright in the driver's seat. Sarah looked up and down the block but didn't see Bunky anywhere. She unlocked the Coiffure's green front door and pushed it open. Whiskey ran into the room and sniffed and sniffed like he was looking for the dogs who had visited yesterday. Sarah turned on the lights and walked through the hinged opening in the counter. She put her backpack in the back room, the salads in the fridge, and the muffins on the table. When she was reaching for her denim paw print apron on the coatrack, the door opened and, for the first time ever, Bunky Buffalo walked into the Coiffure.

"Sarah," he said, speeding toward her, "you've got to help me."

Sarah took a step backwards and Whiskey must have felt her muscles tense and her mind questioning her safety because the dog stepped between her and Bunky and emitted a low-level growl. Just once.

But it was enough for Bunky to hold his hands up, with his palms facing Sarah in the universal sign of surrender.

"It's okay, Whiskey. Good boy,' Sarah said, barely above a whisper. Louder, she said, "Bunky, how can I help you?"

He looked back over his shoulder out the window. His posture was tense, his eyes shifty. Sarah could feel the paranoia rolling off of him like water off a sea otter. She waited for him to answer, but when his eyes kept scanning the outside and he remained silent, she asked, "Would it be better for us to go into the back room?"

His head jerked toward her, his eyes—that looked all pupil and no iris—wide. He nodded his head once.

Sarah walked around him and locked the front door, sending an unspoken prayer that Emily would get there soon. And then the three of them—Bunky, Sarah, and Whisky—went through the hinged counter and into the back room, where the slatted blinds were down and had been turned closed.

Bunky let out an audible breath and collapsed his bulk into a molded plastic, armless chair at the table. Sarah took the chair across from him. Whiskey positioned himself on the floor between Bunky and Sarah, facing Bunky. He was on alert.

Bunky had been staring at his hands or the table, but then raised his head and eyes and looked directly at Sarah. "I'm sorry, but I had nowhere else to go. He told me he'd kill me if I go to the police."

"Who told you not to talk to the police, Bunky?"

"Damien Dragnet."

Sarah's eyes narrowed. She had no idea who that was. "Maybe you should start at the beginning. Who is Damien Dragnet and why is he threatening you?"

Bunky sighed and said, "He's the developer who has been trying to force me to sell my land."

"But you don't want to sell?"

"No. Why would I? It's the only thing I have that was Mama and Daddy's."

Sarah's heart went out to him with the way he worded that, like part of his personality had been arrested in childhood at the death of his father. Sarah sucked in a deep breath and on the exhale said, "Bunky, I have learned that Paul Whitmore was your cousin."

"Yes, he was."

"Do you know why he came back into town?"

Bunky nodded, his eyes fixed on Sarah's. "I called him."

"Had you been in touch with him all of these years?"

"Not really. But I always knew how to reach him, if I needed to. He came back briefly when Mama died. We was close as kids."

"So Paul moved to Cottageville because you asked him to?"

"No. I called him to tell him that Damien dude was pressuring me to sell. But I don't want to. Like I said. And I couldn't anyway. The land is all in a trust and it would take the both of us. That's why I called Paul."

"So you and Paul are the trustees of the Buffalo Brothers Trust?"

Bunky's eyes widened. "You know about the trust?"

"I learned about it as I was investigating Paul's life and death," Sarah admitted.

"See, this is why I came to you. Damien said no police. But I know all about the crimes you've solved and the award from the mayor."

"Thank you for trusting me. So you and Paul are the trustees and you don't want to sell. Did Paul?"

"Nah. I don't think so. His sisters and my daddy are buried in that land."

Sarah was surprised Bunky mentioned Paul's sisters and she decided to try and press her luck. "Was your uncle Milo buried there, too?"

Bunky's eyes were now like saucers and he wasn't blinking. "You know about Uncle Milo?"

"I know he disappeared around age twenty-four."

Bunky fidgeted in his seat and his fingers started moving like a tarantula stretching its hairy legs. Not louder than a whisper, Bunky said, "Milo was killed by Uncle Theo. I guess it don't matter now with almost everyone dead."

Sarah squashed her shock and schooled her face into an expressionless mask. "Why did Uncle Theo kill his brother?"

"Mama said because that first baby girl weren't his. She belong to Milo."

Sarah's mask crumpled when her eyebrows shot to her hairline. "And what happened to that baby girl?"

Bunky squirmed some more in his seat and moved his lips and

released almost no sound. But Sarah saw what words he formed. "Theo killed her, Mama said."

"And the second baby girl?"

Bunky shook his head. "I don't know. No one ever talked about her."

"Is Milo buried on the land?"

"I don't know. When we was little, we were told not to play in the woods 'cause there were ghosts in there. But me and Paul, we never listened. And when we was older, maybe ten and twelve, we found a human skull there. It was dirty and seemed like it had been there a while. We didn't tell anyone and left it right where we found it."

"Were you scared of Uncle Theo?"

Bunky shrugged. "When he was drinking, he weren't very nice. But he taught me to play ball and how to fish and hunt and be a man. He was there when I shot my first buck."

"Do you know why Paul and his mother left and changed their names?"

Bunky nodded his head. "Yeah. Uncle Theo didn't make them too proud to be a Buffalo." His eyes glistened with unshed tears at that statement, and Sarah reached her hand across the table and patted his meaty hand.

"I had wondered if they left because the land held too much sorrow," Sarah admitted.

"That was kinda why Paul didn't want to sell. He liked his life and didn't want the secrets out. Keeping the land meant keeping the secrets."

"I understand," Sarah said. "Though keeping those secrets may have gotten him killed."

"No, Sarah. That's not right. It was his refusing to sell that got him killed, and that's why I might be next...unless I sign these papers from Damien." Bunky pulled some folded and dog-eared papers from inside his plaid wool jacket and started crying for real.

"May I?" Sarah asked, reaching toward the documents.

They were a contract for the sale of two hundred and fifty-eight acres at five thousand dollars an acre, which Sarah was sure was way below market value. The low number made her blood boil. "You can't sign this, Bunky. This is extortion."

"I know." He sniffed. "But I can't not sign it either, unless I want to wind up dead. Damien said what happened to Paul was a warning." And then he cried harder.

Sarah went around the table and wrapped her arms around him, though she didn't know him well. But she felt his pain and the difficulty of his decision. Not to mention the pain and fear that came from decades of keeping secrets to not incur his uncle's wrath.

"I'm going to get you some Kleenexes," Sarah said. She left the breakroom for the bathroom, and while she was pulling tissues from the box, the front door of the Coiffure unlocked and Emily yelled, "Yoohoo," which made Whiskey fly out of the back room barking like the place was on fire.

Sarah approached the counter and whispered to Em, "We have a guest in the back room. Bunky Buffalo. And I have a plan. Can you ring Candace and ask her to come here in plain clothes and to bring Maple?"

Emily's eyes widened and reminded Sarah of a sugar glider's and she nodded her head. "I'm on it."

"Thank you."

Sarah returned to the back room saying as she entered, "That's my assistant Emily Colt." She handed the tissues to Bunky.

He loudly blew his nose before dabbing at his watery eyes.

Sarah seated herself again across from him and reached for his hand. "Bunky, I appreciate you coming here today and for trusting me to help you. I have an idea about how to help you out of this problem and to make sure the party responsible for your cousin's death gets arrested."

"It's Damien. I already told you."

"Yes, I know. But the police will need some proof. Some concrete evidence or for him to admit it." Sarah paused to let that sink in.

"But how are we going to get that?" Bunky asked. "I don't wanna wind up dead. And I don't have much time left. Damien said I had to sign before Thanksgiving, or else." He ran his right pointer finger across his throat like he was slitting it.

"We are going to get Damien to admit what he did to Paul and you are going to get that on tape."

"I'm gonna what?" Bunky's eyes blinked rapidly like he couldn't believe what he just heard. His mouth hung slightly open.

"It will be easy. All we have to do is ask Damien to meet you at your house and when he gets there you can say you don't think the price he's offering is fair. Because let's face it, Bunky, it really isn't. You could get twice as much per acre, maybe a little more."

"But, Sarah, he isn't gonna pay me more when he could just

as easily kill me and then buy the land from the county…" His voice trailed off.

"Do you have a will, Bunky?" Sarah asked as gently as she could.

"Nah. I don't have any family left."

"You don't have to have a family to have a will, Bunky. What if you left your land to the schools or Cottageville Parks or to a charitable organization, someone who would be a good steward of it and not build a mall or subdivisions or a car lot."

"I've never thought of it."

Sarah heard the front door open and Emily and Whiskey greet Candace. She saw Bunky's whole body tense. His eyes darted to the door and around the room like he was looking for a possible escape route. She patted his hand again. "It's okay, Bunky. I asked Candace Grimes to come here."

"But she's a cop," Bunky spat.

"She is, but she and her lop rabbit are clients of ours."

At those words, Candace and Maple stood in the doorway of the breakroom. Candace wore a green and black plaid shirt with a black down vest over top of it and jeans and black motorcycle boots. Maple was snuggled against her chest, wriggling his nose. Whiskey was standing next to Candace with his nose in the air toward Candace's elbow and his rabbit friend. "Sarah. Bunky. What's going on?"

"Take a seat." Sarah motioned. "And let Maple hop around." Then, Sarah filled her friend in on everything Bunky had said, with him interjecting occasionally and Candace interrupting periodically with questions.

Sarah ended with, "I think we should wire Bunky or his house and he should schedule a meeting with Damien and get him to make the confession and the threats again in person where it is recorded and then you'll have the evidence to arrest him."

"That's why you wanted me here? To tell us how to do our jobs?" Candace eyed Sarah.

"No, I wanted you here with your rabbit and plain clothes in case Bunky is being watched."

Bunky's frustration infused every word of "He said if I went to the pigs I'd be bacon."

"Colorful," Candace said with a straight face. "Do you think you are being followed?"

Bunky sighed. "I don't know. Sometimes yes. Other times, I don't think so. Sometimes it is hard to tell. So I've been staying home a lot."

"I think with the right coaching, Bunky can pull this off. I'm willing to work with him on what to say," Sarah said. "If we need to keep the cops away from his house, I think Bill can go in and install a camera in a light fixture and some mics that can't be seen. He oversaw the job at my house. What do you think?" She turned toward Candace.

"I have to bring the Chief in on this."

"Of course you do. But Bunky getting together with friends in town or having them to his house is a lot less suspicious than your panda car in his driveway." Sarah's lips quivered into a glimmer of a smile.

"Understood."

"I'm not sure I like this idea, Sarah," Bunky said.

"Do you have a better one?" Her tone was level, emotionless.

He stared at her for a few beats before admitting he did not.

"So I'll talk to Bill as soon as you both leave. Bunky, expect to see him this morning. Then Jared and I will come over after work and bring you some dinner. We'll go over how to talk to Damien and what to say to get him to confess. And once you feel comfortable enough with that, we'll have you set up the meeting with him and have Candace and her colleagues way out of sight on your property but close enough to arrest him when the time is right. Okay?"

"I'm not sure it is, but I don't think I have another choice. It's either this or die. And I don't wanna die."

Sarah placed her hand over Bunky's again and looked into his eyes. "I don't want you to die either, Bunky."

"Me neither," Candace said. She placed her hand on top of theirs, and just like that they agreed on the plan.

CHAPTER 20

Sarah was thrilled they had mostly small dogs on the schedule for the day. Bunky left in better spirits than he had been in when he walked through the door. Candace and Maple stayed a few minutes longer so it actually looked like the rabbit had an appointment. Sarah called Bill as soon as Candace left to fill him in and to get the microphones and camera installation in motion.

Emily devoured her muffin and started a bath for Sprinkles the shih-tzu, who lived with Cottageville Fire Chief Hannah Beau and her husband Hunter Byrd and their two adopted from China daughters, Bao and Ai. Sprinkles was sweet and spoiled as the only dog belonging to two little girls tended to be. The black and white dog looked gleeful as the shampoo was massaged into its coat.

Sarah texted Jared, "New plans for this evening. Please get the CJ after work and pick up Chinese food and us. We are eating with Bunky Buffalo at his house." Then she told Emily all about her morning.

Jared responded ten minutes later with, "Okay," while Sarah's fingers were creating suds in Charlie the chinook's golden fur. The dog was in the walk-in tub and Whiskey sat against the stainless steel side, providing emotional support, though Sarah wasn't sure that Charlie needed it with his friendly and easy-going personality.

Sarah's thoughts were interrupted by Em asking, "Hey, Sarah, you don't think that Damien person will kill Bunky before all parts of your plan are in place, do you?"

"Umm. I don't think so. He gave Bunky until Thanksgiving to sign the paperwork."

"Yeah, but what if that was just to make him feel more comfortable and to drop his guard?"

Sarah's head jerked and her eyes locked onto her assistant. "Never even occurred to me."

"Do you think there's any way the police can keep an eye on him? Maybe follow him to make sure he doesn't do anything?"

"I don't know. It's not like we have a huge force or that Cottageville is a big place. I think tailing works best in big cities where there's busyness and distractions."

"Maybe you should at least let Candace or Chief James know of the possibility. Damien doesn't sound like a guy who could be trusted to keep his word."

"That's for sure." Once Charlie was out of the tub and onto

a grooming table, Sarah shot a quick text to Candace with Em's concern. Then she toweled the dog before turning on the blow dryer and picking up the brush. He stood stock-still on the table except for leaning into the brush like he loved the feeling of bristles against his skin.

The day went on like this with Sarah going through the motions of the work she loved while feeling like adrenaline was coursing through her body like Ferraris at Formula One. She couldn't wait to get to Bunky's house, to work with him on what to say, and then to spring the trap and get Damien Dragnet arrested for Paul's murder. She wouldn't feel calm until that all came together.

At four-thirty, once all of their clients had been picked up for the day, Sarah turned the "open" sign to "closed" and stood for a moment in the quiet with Whiskey pressed against her right leg. She glanced around the Coiffure, everything was washed, folded, and lined up for tomorrow morning. Sarah caught a glimpse of her reflection in the glass of the front door, "You look like you haven't slept in days," she muttered to herself.

As Whiskey and Sarah stepped outside and closed and locked the front door, Sarah heard the sound of the CJ's oversized tires on the pavement behind her.

"Hey good looking, you need a lift?" Jared said as he exited the Jeep.

Sarah smirked. "Only if you promise to drive fast and recklessly."

"Hmm," Jared said, "I guess I'll get you an Uber then, cause that's not my style. I'm Mr. Smooth and Easy."

"I know, J. That's one of the many things I appreciate about you,"

Sarah said as Jared opened the passenger door for her and Whiskey to jump in.

Whiskey crawled into the back and Sarah slid into the seat and buckled her seatbelt as Jared pulled away from the curve.

Jared was impatient for answers. "Okay, I have the Chinese food and know where we are going, but why? What's going on, Sarah?"

Turning sideways in her seat and looking toward Jared, she said, "I'm not even sure where to begin."

Jared, taking his eyes off the road just long enough to look into Sarah's eyes, said, "Maybe start with how did we get invited to Bunky's house tonight?"

"Bunky showed up at the Coiffure this morning and explained everything to me. And when I say everything, I mean everything. He told me about the family history, what the tension was over, who killed who, why Paul left." Sarah paused then added, "and who killed Paul Whitmore, or should I say Paul Buffalo and why."

"Wait. What? Bunky showed up at your work and volunteered this information?"

"Yes."

"This doesn't sound right, Sarah." Jared's voice trembled.

"Jared, Bunky is so scared. This Damien guy that killed Paul wants to kill him, too. Bunky couldn't go to the police and had no one else to turn to."

In what sounded to Sarah like sarcasm and irritation , Jared said, "And of course he had to go to Sarahlock for help."

"Babe, why are you saying it like that? I haven't done anything wrong." Sarah hated how she sounded defensive.

"I know, I know, I'm sorry. This is all a lot and I don't like that you keep putting yourself in danger."

"Jared, I appreciate your concern, but I think I have a plan that's going to work to catch Paul's killer."

"I'm all ears," Jared said.

"If I can teach Bunky, if I can help him keep his cool and say the right things, I think we can record Damien confessing to the murder. With a little help, I can help Bunky get Damien to say something he shouldn't."

Glancing toward Sarah, Jared said, "And you think it will be that easy?"

Sarah leaned toward Jared and tried to look into his eyes even though he was driving. "Yes. Yes, I do."

"Ugh," Jared sounded exasperated, drumming his fingers on the steering wheel. "Sarah, you do realize this isn't a poodle's haircut gone wrong we're talking about. This is serious. This is dangerous. We are talking about murder and a murderer."

"I know that," Sarah tried for a soft yet reassuring tone. "Bunky trusts me. He doesn't want to sell his property. It's all he has left of his family to remember. And he certainly doesn't want to die. We can help him. We can coach him on what to say."

Jared shook his head. "Sarah, this is the police's job. Why are you trying to run their undercover operations?"

Sarah bit her lip. She'd been expecting this—Jared's protective streak was one of the things she loved about him, but she knew that she couldn't let Jared's fears stand in the way of bringing justice to Paul's death. "I understand your concern, J. I do, but I am only helping

Bunky with what he is going to say when he meets with Damien. Bill set up video cameras and the audio equipment today. The police will be standing by on Bunky's property when Bunky and Damien meet."

Jared was quiet. The rumble of the CJ and an occasional yawn or whimper from Whiskey was the only sound for the next several miles.

"I get it," Jared said. "Bunky can't go to the police, so he goes to you. But there's a big leap between doing some snooping around and trying to trap a killer. You could be putting Bunky, you could be putting all of us in real danger."

Sarah exhaled slowly, "I've thought about it, but not helping feels worse. If this guy Damien gets away with what he did to Paul, he'll keep doing the same to others. And who knows, he could have already done this to many others. It's not fair. It needs to stop. He needs to be stopped."

Jared glanced at her, his brow furrowed. "You should have been a lawyer. You are very convincing." He shook his head with a half-smile. "You are something else, Sarahlock. You are full of heart and want to right wrongs like a superhero."

They both laughed softly as the tension lifted.

The CJ crested the small hill and turned down Bunky's long driveway. It was dark and eerie, like a scene from a zombie apocalypse movie. Whiskey sat up as the Jeep transitioned from gravel road to dirt driveway.

Grabbing Jared's hand on the shifter, Sarah asked, "Are you creeped out, too?"

Playfully repeating Sarah, Jared said, "Am I a little creeped out? No, Sarah, I enjoy being in the middle of nowhere, in pitch black, with killers on the loose. I write graphic novels. I don't need this kind of inspo. I am not the next Stephen King."

Sarah and Jared both laughed as the Jeep came to a stop at the front of Bunky's house. The night was dark. The moon was hiding behind the clouds, so it was nearly impossible to see anything except what the interior lights in the house revealed.

Jared and Sarah opened their doors simultaneously. Jared gently closed his as if not to alert anyone of their arrival. Sarah kept hers open long enough for her furry companion to jump out. Whiskey made his way to a smooth sumac and watered it well. Jared took Sarah's hand and they cautiously walked toward the front door. Sarah carried the take-out. Each step was slow and calculated, like a soldier strategically walking through a mine field, not knowing if the next step could be their last.

Whiskey took a different approach; he seemed to think his humans were playing some kind of game. He jumped around them with playful energy, doing the exact opposite of whatever they were trying to do.

Not amused, Sarah asked, "Whiskey, you nut, what are you doing?"

As the three approached the front door, it slowly opened and they were greeted by an almost inaudible, "Hey, thanks for coming." Bunky opened the door wider, peeked his head out, and glanced from side to side, "Hurry, come in."

The house was filled with a gentle, muted glow—not from ambient lighting, but from light fixtures missing their bulbs. This dim light reminded Sarah of her childhood, particularly the Christmas

Eve mass she once attended. The church was lit just enough to prevent tripping, yet little else was visible. She had felt uneasy then, the same way she did now.

Whiskey slipped away from Sarah's side, his nose twitching as he explored the unfamiliar space, while Bunky guided Sarah and Jared toward the kitchen table, where they could settle in and talk.

Before they were completely seated, Bunky blurted, "I'm really scared, Sarah. I don't know what to do."

Sarah reached across the table and placed her right hand on his left forearm. "I know you are, Bunky. But everything is going to be fine."

"How do you know that?"

Sarah paused and looked intently into Bunky's eyes. She could sense his uncertainty and, being an empath, feel his fear.

As she was formulating her thoughts and words, Jared interjected. "Because we are going to do this together, Bunky."

Sarah continued with Jared's train of thought. "Yes, we are going to do this together. We will work as a team. And Bunky, I know you have felt alone, being up here by yourself and not having family, but you are not alone any more. You have us as family. Jared, Whiskey, Bill, Gladys, Janice, and me, we are your family now and we are going to bring this Damien Dragnet down together."

It was as if a jolt of electricity surged through Bunky. His whole body trembled and tears streamed down his face like the Hoover Dam had just burst open. Bunky's reaction reminded Sarah of the psychosomatic related videos she saw on social media. Even though they were there to catch a murderer, Sarah recognized the importance of this moment in Bunky's healing journey.

Jared slid his chair up against Bunky's and put his long, lean left arm around Bunky's shoulder and pulled him closer. Bunky leaned into Jared's shoulder and wept even louder. Whiskey, treating Bunky like a hurting furry friend at the Coiffure, sat at Bunky's feet, with his furry head on Bunky's knee.

Sarah's hand rested gently on Bunky's arm, while Jared kept holding onto the stranger he barely knew. Sarah witnessed a side of Jared she had never noticed before. She always knew he was kind and compassionate, but now she saw a tenderness and sincerity in him that was completely new. She already loved this tall, artistic man, yet something in her heart changed. It felt impossible, but her love for Jared deepened even more.

Bunky drew in a long, deliberate breath, then released it in a deep aching moan, the kind that echoed with the heaviness of loss. Whiskey yelped in surprise, his ears twitching at the sudden sound. Without warning, Bunky sat up and muttered, "Excuse me."

Jared eased his chair back to its original place as Bunky rose and made his way across the kitchen toward a half-bath. Whiskey trailed after him, faithful and alert, until the door clicked shut. Whiskey settled at his post outside the bathroom door, as if standing guard over a wounded soul.

Across the table, Sarah and Jared's eyes locked. They didn't speak; there was no need to. The silence between them said everything.

CHAPTER 21

Bunky lingered in the bathroom for what felt like an eternity. Behind the closed door came the muffled sound of grief—sobs, the crumple of tissue after tissue, the sniffling of a heart trying to mend itself with tears and tissue. At last, after what must've been ten minutes, the door creaked open. Bunky stepped out, his weathered face blotched and weary, but his eyes steadier, like a storm had passed but now he saw the sun. He cleared his throat, squared his forward slumping shoulders, and said in a voice roughened by emotion, "Alright, we's got work to do."

Whiskey, following right behind him, gave a "woof-woof" as if he were in agreement.

Simultaneously standing, Jared and Sarah began stepping away from the kitchen table. "Show us where Bill installed the cameras," Sarah said as she peeked her head from the kitchen to the living room.

Bunky walked past them and into the living room. "That ole man's handier than a Swiss army pocket knife. He and them ladies got the whole place wired up like somethin' out of a spy movie."

Jared raised an eyebrow. "Bill?"

Bunky chuckled, though it came out more nervous than amused. "Yes, Bill. But it weren't Bill that ran the show. It were that woman Janice."

Whiskey barked once, short and sharp, as if recognizing his friend's name.

Bunky belly laughed. "See, Whiskey knows who runs the show. That Janice lady."

Sarah smiled, "Janice knows her stuff, that's for sure. I am glad she was able to help Bill."

"Help Bill?" Bunky took a deep breath and scratched his belly. "I don't think you gets what I am saying. When they arrived, I was thinkin' Bill was the boss and things, you know, no offense little lady, but he be the man. That's what I were thinkin'. But as soon as they come in, Janice started talkin' like she were trained by the FBI or something. 'We'll need one here,' she says, pointing to the top corner of the door. 'Line of sights good, but mind the glare from the window. Need another one over the armoire. One in the hallway for coverage of both exits.' I tell ya, she talked about angles and escape routes and blind spots, like she been doin' this her whole life."

Jared chuckled. "You have no idea, Bunky, you have no idea."

"I do now," Bunky exclaimed as he shook his head. "She even told Mr. Bill where to mount the router so it's get the best signal through the house. Bill just nodded and said, 'Yes, ma'am, like he was taking orders. I don't even know what a router is."

Amused by Bunky's narrative, Sarah inquired, "And where was Gladys during all of this?"

"Gladys didn't say much. She just watched and smiled. She the quiet type. Her eyes, her eyes, always be moving though. She noticed everythin'. Made me a little nervous if I'm honest."

Sarah exchanged a glance with Jared. "Sounds like quite a crew."

"Oh, they was somethin' for sure," Bunky said, motioning for them to follow.

The living room was ordinary, old, and musty. The tattered lace curtains landed on the old pine floors. The floorboards leading into the house were dark and stained, like someone spilled motor oil and left it. The place looked uninhabited. The bookshelves were lined with dusty hardbacks and Bibles, a recliner with protruding springs was draped with a Christmas quilt, and pictureless picture frames with broken glass hung on the walls.

Bunky reached up and pointed to a small black dot nestled unsuspiciously near the crown molding. "That's a camera?" Sarah asked.

"Sure is," Bunky proudly responded. "Got five of 'em in total. This one here, one by the back door, one over the front door, one up yonder by the hallway, and"....walking over to the piece of furniture across the room, "got one hidden above the armoire."

Whiskey padded over, sniffed the base of the armoire, and gave a deep "woof," as if confirming Bill's spy work.

Sarah giggled. "Glad you approve, Whisk."

Jared shifted his weight from his left foot to the right. "I know the cameras are in place, but what's the plan?"

Turning toward Jared, Sarah said, "That's what Bunky and I are going to work on now."

Bunky's eyes darted toward Sarah, "Yeah, Sarah, cause I'm still scared. This Damien got evil in him. He is mean as a snake and twice as slippery, too. I don't wanna end up like Paul." He swallowed hard. "Nobody deserves to be hanged."

Sarah began to speak, "Bunky..."

But Bunky interrupted, "I ain't scared of much, snakes, wolves, bears, hard work, whatever, but that man, he's a different type of fella."

Jared frowned. "I'm sure all of this is overwhelming, Bunky. Actually, it's scary. I'm scared too, and I'm not in your shoes."

"It is scary, but we are all in this together," Sarah interjected. "Remember, everything is being recorded and the police will be hiding on your property."

Bunky gave a nervous chuckle. "I just don't wanna end up hangin' from no tree like poor Paul."

Sarah's tone was firm, when she said, "Bunky, listen to me. Janice knows what she is doing because she's done this sort of thing before and so has Bill. The police are trained in this type of stuff. Jared and I have watched them take down criminals in the past. You are going to be safe. All you have to do is get Damien to confess to killing Paul."

Bunky shifted his weight from his heels to the balls of his feet back to his heels, clearly uncomfortable. "Why do you think it will be easy?"

Jared placed a steady hand on Bunky's shoulder.

Sarah smiled, admiring this nurturing side of Jared, "It's going to be easy because Damien is an evil, power hungry man. His own arrogance will cause his downfall. I remember hearing 'Pride comes before destruction, and haughty spirit before a fall.' When you meet with Damien, let his pride lead to his demise."

"I'm not sure what you mean, Sarah, but I do believe you."

"Hey," Jared said, "I'm starving. Let's go back into the kitchen and dive into the Chinese food we brought and discuss the plan."

Within five minutes, the table was cluttered with takeout containers—lo mein, egg rolls, fried rice, beef and broccoli, and General Tso's chicken.

Picking up a carton, Sarah asked, "Bunky, do you want the rest of the beef and broccoli?"

"Nah, can't eat much knowin' what's comin'."

Jared reached over and patted Bunky's forearm. "This will all be over soon."

"That's right," Sarah chimed in. "Damien will be behind bars before Thanksgiving. For men like this jerk, their power is their oxygen. Pride's their weakness. When you meet with him, if he thinks you are scared and broken, he'll puff himself up. He will want to show you he's the reason you are scared, he's the reason Paul is gone. He will do everything in his power to make you feel small."

Clearly not understanding, Bunky muttered, "So?"

Speaking with confidence, like she was on Jeopardy and was one hundred percent sure of her answer, Sarah said, "So....we are going to play into his game. When Damien comes, act tired. Defeated. Tell him you've been thinking maybe he's right, maybe selling the farm is the smart thing. But then say that you keep hearing Paul's voice in your head, telling you not to sell. That will trigger him for sure."

Looking at Sarah like an eighth grader learning algebra for the first time, Bunky questioned, "Trigger him how?"

"He will want to prove to you Paul's voice doesn't matter. That Paul is dead and you will be too if you don't sell. It's a pride thing. Damien wants to have control over your feelings."

Jared spoke up, "He'll slip. Guys like that always do." Jared's voice trailed off..."atleast on TV they do."

Nodding slowly, Bunky asked, "Wait, do I bait him or am I the bait? Cause I feel like I'm the bait."

Sarah chuckled. "You calling him to tell him to meet you here is the bait. You telling him you are thinking of selling is the bait."

Rubbing his chin with oily fingers from the egg rolls, Bunky said, "So I bait him. Tell him I'm thinkin' about sellin' this here land. Then I let him do the talkin'."

"Yes, exactly. And when he starts talking, don't interrupt. Let him run his mouth. And play into it. Act scared, but don't go overboard."

Bunky half-smiled "You think I will be acting scared? Heck no, I will be real scared."

All three humans in the room had a good chuckle. Whiskey

added two "ruff, ruff," and a hearty tail wag.

Jared reached his long arms high above his head and leaned back in the kitchen chair to get a good stretch. Through a yawn came a muffled, "It's getting late, we need to wrap this up."

"Oh hun, it is and you need to get up early for work," Sarah said, looking at her watch.

Bringing his arms down from overhead, Jared glanced at his watch, "You guys can practice what Bunky is going to say for about ten minutes, longer than that, I will be asleep right here at the kitchen table."

Sarah leaned toward Bunky, "Okay Bunky, let's practice."

Bunky groaned, "I ain't no actor and I ain't too smart to be learning a bunch of lines."

Like a middle school teacher speaking to a hardheaded student, Sarah said, "You don't need to be either. Just feel it and let Damien talk."

Bunky took a deep breath and lowered his head. "Damien.....I been thinkin' about your offer. Maybe it's time to let the old farm go." Bunky paused. "You know, I can't sleep none since Paul, since Paul, well you know, since Paul died."

Sarah pretended to be Damien, "Paul was a fool to stand in my way."

Bunky raised his head enough to make eye contact with Sarah, "What do you mean a fool to stand in your way? You mean you, umm, you...?"

Sarah stood up and looked down at Bunky, "Yes, you idiot. I took care of him just like I will take care of you if you don't sell me your farm."

Jared quickly interjected, "And once he admits to killing Paul, don't celebrate. Don't smile. Heck, don't even blink. Just hang your head and keep acting weak."

Jared stood and started cleaning the kitchen table. He gathered the to-go containers and paper plates and placed them in an overflowing kitchen trash can while Bunky and Sarah talked a little more about potential conversations between Bunky and Damien.

"You got this, Bunky," Sarah said with confidence in her voice.

Jared slipped his arm around Sarah's waist, "Yes, you got this. The cameras are in place. You know what to say. The police will be hiding on your property. Everything will go smoothly and justice will be served."

"Amen to that," Sarah said as she kissed Jared on the cheek.

"Let's go home, Whiskey, I've got to get up in a few hours," Jared said as he pulled Sarah from the hip to exit the kitchen.

"Thank you for comin' and for helpin' me. It feels good knowin' I ain't alone in this."

"You are not alone." Sara smiled and side-hugged Bunky. "I will call you tomorrow to go over everything again and discuss the final plans before you call Damien to meet." She put his number in her phone.

"Okay. Thank you."

As Bunky opened the front door, Whiskey practically ran through Sarah's legs to exit the house and revisit the smooth sumac he christened when they arrived.

"That's a good boy, finish your duty and get in the Jeep," Jared said as he opened Sarah's door.

"Thank you, my lord."

"Of course, mi'lady," Jared responded as he leaned down to kiss Sarah.

Their kiss was interrupted, as Whiskey squirmed past them and jumped into the front passenger seat of the CJ.

"In the back, silly dog," Sarah said, pointing to the back seat. Whiskey let out one gruff "ruff" and crawled to the back.

Sarah settled into her seat as Jared closed the door behind her. He then crossed in front of the Jeep and walked to the driver's side door. Sliding into his seat, he shut the door, and cranked the motor. As the Jeep reversed down the driveway, Sarah gave one final wave to Bunky before he closed the front door.

"Jared, everything's going to be okay, right?"

Jared turned around, glancing between the two front seats as he carefully steered the CJ down the long, dark driveway. A tense silence filled the air. Sarah felt the tires transition from the dirt driveway onto the gravel road as Jared cut the wheel hard to the left.

"Yes, I believe so. Damien's arrogance will be his demise," Jared replied, shifting the Jeep into first gear and releasing the clutch.

CHAPTER 22

Sarah felt like a Chihuahua, as her body was filled with anxious energy as she left her house for the morning's walk. A leashless Whiskey led Sarah on his usual route, up the street, through the park, and onto Main Street, stopping by his buddy Bill's house to snag a treat.

"Morning, Bill," Sarah called as Whiskey bounded up Bill's front steps and sat at his feet and extended his paw for a handshake.

Bill shook Whiskey's paw, then handed him a chicken biscuit from his gallon size glass jar.

"Top of the morning to you, Sarah," Bill said as he rubbed in between Whiskey's ears. "How did last night go?"

"I think it went well, but Bunky is scared. I'm not sure how he can't be, when he's inviting his cousin's killer to his house."

"Yeah, Sarah, I get it. How do you prepare mentally for something like that?"

"It makes me angry, nauseated, and sad all at the same time," Sarah punctuated the words with her right closed fist banging on the handrail.

With a gentle grandfatherly facial expression, Bill said, "I get it, Sarah. Injustice cuts deep, not just because something unfair happened but because it tells the heart that truth and goodness didn't seem to matter."

"Bill, you are so right. And that is exactly why Damien must be caught. It angers me that some rich, power-hungry city-slicker can bully the people in our little town." Banging her closed fist on the hand rail again, Sarah continued, "Things like this make me question why some people can harm others and walk away like nothing happened. And for what? Money? Fame? Power?" She mimed vomiting. "We are going to do whatever it takes for things to be made right and for justice to prevail."

Bill sat up in his chair and began clapping. "Bravo, bravo, you have my vote in the next elections for governor."

Whiskey must have thought the applause was for him because he circled in front of Bill's chair.

Blushing, Sarah said, "You are funny, Bill. I guess I will step off my righteous soap box for now and go back to being a humble dog groomer."

"Don't be silly, Sarah. Don't ever stop fighting for justice and truth. You keep being you."

"Thanks, Bill. Now you know why we stop here everyday...your kindness makes Whiskey and my days better."

With a beaming smile, Bill said, "I love you both."

"Thanks, we love you to the moon and back. Right, Whiskey?"

"Ruff," responded Whiskey.

"By the way, great job installing the spy cams," Sarah said.

Bill chuckled, "I simply followed orders and did exactly what I was told."

Sarah put her right foot on the bottom stair. "Bunky said Janice ran the show and seemed to know a lot of spy type stuff."

"Bunky is not wrong in his assessment," Bill remarked with a teeth-revealing smile.

"Let's go, Whisk," Sarah called. "Thanks for the chat and Whiskey's treat. I'm sure we will be in touch soon."

"Have a good day."

Sarah and Whiskey crossed the street and headed south half a block before Sarah pulled open the red door to Java and Juice. The bell above the door chimed, and Mayor Trisha and her BFF, Barbara, were seated at their usual table.

Sarah and the women exchanged good mornings as Whiskey beelined to the counter where Jared was manning the register. Jared leaned over the counter with his hand outstretched, "Paw me five," Jared commanded before retracting his arm. "Good boy."

Whiskey sat on his hind legs and raised his body off his hind legs with his front legs and paws extended in front of his body. Looking at Jared, Whiskey let out a "grraaaa."

"What in the world, dog, you look like a kangaroo," exclaimed Jared, as he tossed Whiskey a homemade chicken dog biscuit.

"Mi'lady, what can I get for you?" Jared reached for Sarah's to-go tumbler, but Sarah pulled it away.

"The coffee can wait. I want a kiss."

"Mi'lady, I believe I can fulfill your order," Jared said as he leaned over the counter, gently placed his hands on the sides of Sarah's face, and placed his lips on hers.

"Thank you, my lord, now you can fill my tumbler," Sarah said with a giddy giggle.

Jared turned to fill the tumbler with Sarah's favorite dark roast coffee, leaving no room for cream. Then he used tongs to remove two peach and cinnamon muffins with a cream cheese frosting from the pastry display and placed them in a Java and Juice bag. "Babe, do you want pumpkin salads with grilled chicken and honeyed ricotta or would you prefer the spinach salad with honeycrisp apples, cranberries, pecans, and goat cheese?"

"Oh my gosh, they both sound delicious, but I will take two spinach salads."

Jared pulled two salads from the fridge, one for Emily and one for Sarah. He rang up the total on the register and Sarah tapped her card and left her usually twenty percent tip.

"I wish you'd quit doing that," expressed Jared."

Sarah pinched the sides of her jeans as though lifting a skirt and dipped into a playful curtsy for Jared. "You deserve it, my lord."

"You are ridiculous, Sarah Carter. Now get out of here before I have to call the police."

Whiskey and Sarah exited Java and Juice and hurried down the street to Carter's Canine Coiffure. Emotionally drained and not having consumed enough caffeine yet, Sarah unlocked the green front door and made her way to the counter, while Whiskey parked himself at the base of the counter, facing the front entrance. As she was setting the Java and Juice bag containing the muffins on the counter, in walked Emily, who seemed more festive than ever. On her lower half, she wore her black Doc Marten Mary Jane's, with a pair of brown, orange, and yellow turkey cartoon socks pulled high over black tights. Up top, she donned a faded and cropped burnt-orange crewneck sweatshirt over a long white t-shirt that hung out far below the crew. Her two pig tails hung out beneath the black beanie on her head.

"Hey Ems, I am loving the outfit today."

"Thanks. I'd love to say I went with a different vibe today, but the truth is, I lost a bet with Travis. That's why I'm rocking the turkey socks. Once I was stuck with these." Emily held her foot up so Sarah could see the socks well. "I figured I might as well lean in and go full festive mode."

"Might I dare ask what kind of bet?" Sarah asked, arching a brow.

"Ugh, don't remind me." Em groaned. "Travis bet he could beat me at Mario Kart. If I lost, I had to wear a pair of his dad's ridiculous Thanksgiving socks. I said, 'game on' because I never lose at Mario. Well, turns out, I did."

"Well, Em, you are a good sport. And you look cute, too."

Knocking on the door triggered Whiskey to race barking toward it. Sarah could see Chief James through the glass. She went back through the hinged counter and opened the door. "Good morning, Chief."

He bent over and scratched Whiskey's ears before straightening and saying to Sarah, "You organizing undercover operations now? I thought I told you to stay out of Paul Whitmore's death."

"You did, Chief James. But Bunky Buffalo came to me. I've only been looking into Paul's life. I swear."

"Grimes thinks your plan is solid, if Bunky keeps his cool and can get Damien talking. I put out some feelers in other communities where he's built. There have been some rumors..." Chief James didn't finish his thought, but his eyes held Sarah's like he was telepathically trying to get his point across.

"Bunky is ready. We role played last night until he was comfortable."

"That's good to know. Do you know when he's asking for the meeting?"

Sarah shook her head no. "I told him I'd call him today. I figure the sooner the better. Does that work for you?"

"Nice of you to check." Sarcasm oozed from Chief James.

Sarah's first inclination was to apologize, but she squashed that down. It wasn't her fault Bunky came to her or that Damien threatened to kill him if he went to the police. She squared her shoulders and met Chief James' eyes. She said nothing.

"Let me know as soon as you talk to Bunky, Sarah. I mean it. We need to make sure nothing can go wrong with this plan."

"I get that. Bunky's life is riding on it. And the health and safety of our community."

"Exactly." With that one word, the chief turned on his heel and walked out the door.

After Sarah locked the door again, Emily piped up, "Tense much? Gees. Give him a lump of coal and he could poop a diamond."

Sarah cracked up at that image. She laughed so hard her abdomen hurt and tears trickled down her cheeks. Emily laughed with her. When Sarah caught her breath, she said, "Oh my. Thank you. I needed that."

"You're welcome. So things went well with Bunky?"

"Yes. Once we worked through his fear. Until we were out there, I never realized how alone he must feel. I know the rumors say he drinks too much, but who really knows much about him? He keeps to himself and mostly lives in the periphery. Maybe it's time for that to change, if he wants. Jared and I made it clear we are here for him and want to be his friend."

"Aww, that's so nice of you, but I would expect nothing less."

Sarah and Emily finished their muffins just as body builder and entrepreneur Tony tried the door handle. Sarah rushed to unlock the door and let him and Spike, his seventy-five pound pit bull, inside. Whiskey ran to greet his friend. "Hey, Big T. How's your empire building?"

"Going well, Sarah. Just opened my tenth fitness center. We weren't here for the Halloween parade, but I heard you found a body."

"I did. And very soon we'll catch the killer." Sarah couldn't have stopped the grin on her face if she'd tried—it spread like sunshine breaking through clouds after a week of rain.

"That's good. I'm sure you will."

"Does Spike need anything special today?" Emily asked, taking his leash from Tony. Sometimes Spike came to them in preparation for photo shoots as he was as much a part of the Big T's Fitness brand as Tony.

"If you could use the anti-itch shampoo, we'd both appreciate it. Thank you. I'll be back in a couple of hours." With that, Tony left the Coiffure and Emily guided Spike into a walk-in tub. Whiskey parked himself against the tub for emotional support.

Sarah's cell phone rang with an unknown number. She debated whether or not to answer but her curiosity won. "Hello."

"Sarah, it's Bunky. I'm meeting him Saturday morning at ten."

"Okay. Thank you for letting me know."

"You need to be here. I don't wanna be alone."

"You mean on Saturday?"

"Yes. Come early and then hide in a bedroom or somewheres. I can't do this without you."

"Ummm, okay. I'll be there between eight and eight-thirty, just in case he shows early."

"Thank you." Bunky's voice sounded strained, like he was holding back strong emotions. "I'll keep practicing what you said."

"Do you need to get together again and rehearse?" Sarah wasn't sure that was wise, but she wanted him to be confident and to pull this off.

"Nah. It's okay." With those three words, he disconnected.

Sarah stared at her phone for a moment before texting Chief James and Officer Grimes. "Damien meeting Saturday at 10 a.m. at B's."

She paused as she saw the telltale three dots of someone composing a message.

"Roger that," Grimes responded.

"He wants me there," Sarah texted.

Her phone rang almost immediately. "Absolutely not," Chief James' voice boomed through the microphone.

"I have reservations, too, Chief. But he told me he can't do this alone." Sarah hated how the pitch of her voice raised. She breathed deeply, trying to ground better.

"You can't be there. It's too big a risk."

"I understand. But I'm not sure Bunky will go through with it without me. It's like I'm his emotional support animal... or maybe his first friend in a very long time." Sarah blew out an exasperated sigh. "I know the risks. I will get there two hours early and hide and not make a sound."

"I could just arrest you so you couldn't do it," Chief James threatened.

"On what grounds?" Sarah shot back. "I won't be trespassing. I've been invited."

"Interfering in a police operation."

Sarah shouted, "There wouldn't be a police operation if I hadn't come up with this plan and set it in motion."

Whiskey whimpered and ran to his human and nipped at her calf.

She heard a huge sigh come through the phone before the Chief said in a low voice, "Okay, Sarah. You win. But we do this my way. I want you in a vest. I want to pick your hiding place. And I don't want you to come out until we tell you it is all-clear. Get it?"

"Yes, sir. Thank you, sir."

"Don't make me regret this," he said. "I'll see you at Bunky's house at seven-thirty Saturday morning. Let him know." And he then disconnected.

Sarah shoved her phone into the back pocket of her jeans. She was literally vibrating like a speaker where the bass was cranked to maximum.

"OMG, Sarah. I've never heard you yell at Chief James before... or anyone for that matter. Are you okay?" Emily asked. She was elbows deep in shampoo suds.

"I am for now. Having push-back from Chief James was expected and that probably pales to what I am going to hear from Jared. You know how worried and protective he is over me."

"Rightfully so. Are you sure you want to be there when Bunky talks to a confessed killer? What if he murders Bunky while you're in the house? What are you going to do, Sarah?"

"I don't know. All I know is Bunky doesn't want to do this alone, and I promised to be there for him. I'll figure it out and I'll keep myself safe. No one will know I'm in the house except him, me, Jared, and the police."

"And me," Emily added.

"Yes, and you. But you'd never rat me out." Sarah smiled at her assistant. "You love me," she joked.

"Well, yes, and I also need this job." Emily cackled at her own comment.

Sarah shook her head at Emily before ducking into the bathroom and texting Moose McCabe, Cottageville's most popular lawyer, asking him to update her will, just in case, giving the Coiffure to Emily Colt and her house and Whiskey to Jared Greene. "Can you do it before end of day? I'll stop to sign on my way home."

"My assistant will have it at the desk, along with the bill," he responded.

"Thanks," Sarah wrote, praying no one would need to disclose its contents for decades.

CHAPTER 23

Jared and Sarah dropped Whiskey off to play with Cassatt and Kahlo at seven on Saturday morning, where Bill, Janice, and Gladys were all gathered over coffee and pastries from Java and Juice. The three octogenarians wished Sarah well and said they looked forward to hearing all about how it went when she returned to pick up her dog.

"We'll have lunch waiting, dear," Gladys said.

"Thank you," Sarah said before kissing her cheek. She hugged Bill and Janice before saying good-bye.

Jared had said repeatedly how he wasn't comfortable with what was about to go down. How he wished Sarah wasn't going to be in the house. But on the drive to Bunky's he skipped all of the things he had said for the past two days and told Sarah how proud he was of her and how much he loved her. She held his hand as they drove.

At seven-thirty, he dropped Sarah off at Bunky's front door, and then he drove a mile down the road, made a left down a dirt road and cut through a field until he came to an old barn that had seen better days. His car wasn't visible from any roads so he parked it to the left of the building. Inside the building were all of the police vehicles Cottageville owned, along with all of the uniformed officers, except for their Chief. Jared said hi to Beams and Grimes and then tried to fade into the background while they did their prep. He was grateful they permitted him to be in this space. In one of the police SUVs, Jared could hear the audio being transmitted from the house. A police officer Jared didn't know sat in the backseat with a computer screen in his lap watching the cameras.

Chief James had entered the back door of Bunky's house as Sarah entered the front. He met her in the kitchen and handed her a Kevlar vest. "Bunky, do you know exactly what to say?" he asked.

"Yes. Try to negotiate more money. Act wimpy so he seems more powerful. Talk about Paul. I got it." Bunky offered them both cups of coffee, but Chief James declined.

Sarah asked for half a cup. She really didn't need any more caffeine coursing through her system; the adrenaline was enough. But she wanted something to do with her hands, to keep her from picking at her nails or any of her other nervous habits. The warmth of the liquid in the mug took the chill from her fingers.

"Show me around," Chief James said to Bunky.

In plain clothes, Candace had visited the day before and drew a schematic of the house so they knew the layout and all of the access points for when they would need them. But Chief James had never been inside the Buffalo farmhouse.

Bunky pointed to a powder room off a short hallway at the back of the house. Then he led them from the kitchen through the dining room and into the living room. One room was off the living room and that was a bedroom with a small attached bath. Up the stairs from the living room ran a hallway with doors to three bedrooms and one full bathroom with a claw footed tub.

Chief James opened every armoire and closet door, peeked under each bed, and looked out every window at the view. As they descended the stairs, he said, "Sarah, I want you in the room downstairs, in the bathroom against the toilet side wall. That way you can't be seen by any window. Stay there and don't move—"

Just then the radio near Chief James' shoulder crackled. "Truck approaching. Get out now."

"What?!" Bunky's eyes looked like they were popping out of his head as Sarah and the Chief raced to the back room. Chief James opened a window and launched himself through the opening.

Sarah quickly shut it and shooed Bunky away. "Go," she whispered. "Sounds like it is show time. You'll do fine. Now go. Answer the door."

He gave her one long look as she flattened her back to the wall. He huffed out a breath and then lumbered out of the bedroom.

Sarah waited a few breaths and willed her heart to beat quieter as it seemed so loud in her ears. Then she heard the front door open and

Bunky said, "You're early. Really early. I thought we said ten."

Damien laughed but didn't sound amused. "You don't sound happy to see me."

"No. I mean yes. I mean, it's fine." Bunky stumbled over the words.

Sarah tried to send him some peace.

"I was having my morning coffee. You want a cup?"

"No, what I want is your signature on the papers."

Sarah heard what sounded like boots on the hardwood floor.

"I know. I know," Bunky said. "But I was thinking, maybe five thousand an acre isn't enough. I looked at other places for sale and what they are going for—"

Damien cut him off. "Five thousand is a fair price." His voice seethed with anger.

"But Paul said—"

"Paul doesn't know crap. And he's dead anyway. Look what happened to him. Drugged and hung and dressed up like a spectacle—"

Bunky interrupted. "He was drugged?" Incredulousness rang through those three words.

"Of course he was. How else was I supposed to get him to cooperate." Ego oozed from Damien.

"You killed him?" Bunky sounded pissed.

"I told you. It was a warning and worse would happen to you if you don't sign those damn papers." Damien was screaming now.

And Bunky shouted back, "How dare you pull a gun on me!"

Sarah's heart felt like it stopped in her chest. She didn't know if she should stay hidden or jump out to help Bunky.

But it didn't matter because suddenly she heard the front and back doors slam open and "Police! Drop your weapon!" At the same time, she heard a gun discharge and Bunky's piercing scream. Followed by Candace Grimes' voice saying, "This is unit 278. One down, GSW, Requesting Code 3 at the Buffalo farm. Scene is secure."

At the words, "Scene is secure," Sarah knew it was safe to leave her hiding place. She crept into the bedroom and peered out the doorway right and left before walking into the living room. Between the dining room and the kitchen, Officer Beams had Damien Dragnet face down on the ground with his hands cuffed behind him. Damien was muttering and cursing as Beams told him anything he said can and would be used against him in a court of law. Damien spit at the floor on that statement.

"You're disgusting," Officer Beams said, jerking his handcuffs to punctuate his opinion.

Bunky was sitting on the kitchen floor with his hand over his bicep, blood gushing between his fingers. Grimes was squatting next to him, talking to him softly.

Sarah hurried toward them. "Bunky, are you okay?"

"I am, Sarah. I tried to do what you said and give him power, but he made me so angry. I couldn't let him get away with it. And then he pulled out the gun."

Sarah stood behind him and placed her hands on his shoulders. "I know, Bunky. You were amazing. I can't believe you got shot."

"He isn't feeling it yet because of all of the adrenaline," Grimes said. "But the bullet didn't hit any bone or tendons. It's really a knick that with some stitches and some painkillers, he'll be fine."

"Thank God," Sarah said. "Bunky, I'm proud of you. You were so brave. And you saved your farm."

Through the open front door, Sarah could see the ambulance and two police cars pulling up to the front of the house. Beams escorted Damien Dragnet, who was still mumbling threats and obscenities, out to a waiting patrol car. The Parks entered the house with their medic bags. They took Bunky's vitals and looked at his wound, before asking if he felt well enough to walk to their vehicle or if they should get the chair.

Jared came through the back door of Bunky's house and wrapped his arms around Sarah's waist and rested his chin on her shoulder. "He had me so worried for a minute."

"Me too," Sarah whispered, kissing his cheek.

"Did you stay hidden?"

"I did. I promised you and Chief James I would and I did. Until after the police busted through the doors and made the arrest."

"Thank you, love. Knowing that makes me feel so much better." Jared squeezed her tighter.

Sarah looked around the officers who were doing their jobs photographing the scene, securing the gun, and locating the bullet. She pulled on the Velcro holding her Kevlar vest together and passed it to Grimes. "Thank you for bringing this together and for believing in my plan."

"It's always good when it comes together and is executed almost flawlessly...or in this case well enough." Grimes chuckled. "What matters most is we got our man and he confessed."

Sarah nodded her head. "I'm glad it worked out and that I

fulfilled the promise I made to Paul on Halloween: to find his killer."

"We may need an official statement from you later, even though we have the tapes," Chief James reminded Sarah as she and Jared were leaving through the back door.

"Sounds good. Thank you for permitting me to be a part of this." And in an uncharacteristic move, Sarah grabbed Chief James and gave him a hug.

His eyes went wide and his mouth formed an O.

"Not much surprises him," Grimes said. "Way to catch him off guard." Her grin showed her teeth.

"Come on, Sarahlock. Let's go get Watson and go home," Jared said, pulling her across the acreage toward the barn that was barely visible from the house.

CHAPTER 24

On Thanksgiving morning, Java and Juice was closed for the holiday, but Jared and Sarah were busy inside the cafe rearranging chairs and tables, grouping them together into bigger communal configurations. They had decided to host a holiday potluck for anyone in Cottageville who wanted to come or who had nowhere else to go and Ginger graciously offered them the space. Three turkeys were roasting in the cafe's commercial ovens as they were Jared and Sarah's contributions to the celebration. The festivities were to begin at two, and Sarah was busy creating flower and leaf arrangements in small glass vases and bottles she found in a thrift store. Gold and orange marigolds, bright yellow and Mexican red sunflowers, purple dahlia, and rust-colored mums flirted with fern, baby's breath, and eucalyptus in each centerpiece.

Earlier in the day, Jared and Bill had put a banquet table against the far wall and covered it with white tablecloth. This would serve as the buffet table. Cans of sterno and some steel serving trays waited to keep the food warm once everyone arrived. A stack of mismatched platters and crockpots was already starting to accumulate at one end—early contributions from townsfolk who couldn't resist dropping things off ahead of time. The comforting smells of roasting turkey mingled with hints of cinnamon and nutmeg from the pumpkin pies cooling on the counter, wrapping the café in a warmth that felt like home itself.

Whiskey lay near the door, chin resting on his paws, his eyes following Sarah's every move. Outside, the wind tossed a few stubborn leaves down Main Street, but inside Java and Juice, the world felt safe, expectant, and full of gratitude. Sarah paused to take it all in—the cozy chaos, the colors, the scents—and thought that this, right here, was what community really meant.

A few minutes before two, Sarah propped the door open and greeted their first guests, Bill, Janice, Gladys, and the poodles. Over Bill's shoulder was a six bottle tote bag filled with wine. And he carried two pecan pies that Gladys had made. Janice was trailed by a wagon with a 12-quart pot of mashed potatoes.

"Oh my," Sarah said when she saw the white mountain of spuds. "You really are feeding the town."

"Can't let anyone go hungry," Mrs. Jenkins said.

"Of course not," Sarah agreed. She removed the pot from the

wagon so that Jared could park the wagon in the kitchen out of the way of traffic. She carried the pot to the buffet table.

Candace Grimes was the next to arrive, and she walked in with Bunky Buffalo whose arm was still wrapped and in a sling to prevent him from moving his arm too much while it healed. Sarah gave them each a hug, though she embraced Bunky gingerly so as not to cause him any more pain. He handed Sarah a plastic sack from Produce and More that contained two bags of salad kits.

"Thank you," Sarah said. "These will be tasty. Help yourself to some drinks."

Sarah carried the bags of salad toward the kitchen so she could get a big bowl for it. While she was mixing the salad, Jared popped up on her left and said, "Chief James and Barbara just arrived. Did you know they were coming?"

"Nope," Sarah said, "but the more the merrier. Is Sascha with them?"

"I don't think so." Jared grabbed a gallon jug of apple juice he had bought and carried it through the swinging double doors to the cafe. He poured two cups of it for Ai and Bao, and offered it to their parents Hunter and Hannah, who said they preferred more adult beverages. "I'm not on call today," Hannah said, "and neither is Chief James, so get him a glass of something too." Her smile lit up her whole face.

"Okay, Two adult beverages coming up," Jared said, going into bartending mode by uncorking wine and pouring.

Sarah giggled at him. Then movement at the door caught her eye. Daphne Smith, wearing her long black leather coat open in the front, over a cream cashmere sweater and black wool trousers, entered the cafe. Pierre's designer leather leash was in her right hand. Over her shoulder was a designer tote bag. "*Bonjour*, Sarah. *Je te souhaite un joyeux Action de Grâce!*"

"*Bonjour, Daphné. Bonjour, Pierre*," Sarah said. "*Bienvenue à notre fête!*"

Daphne's happiness at Sarah speaking French was evident in the way she was beaming. "*Bien.*" She dragged out the word in her enthusiasm, before reaching into her tote bag and pulling out an effigy of Whiskey and presenting it to Whiskey.

Sarah felt like all of the oxygen had been sucked from the room. She knew her eyes were huge and her mouth was agape. At least half the room had stopped their conversations and were staring at them. "You made this?" Sarah squeaked.

"*Oui.*" Daphne's eyes sparkled as they admired the mini-Whiskey on the palm of her hand.

"You made all of them?" Sarah asked.

"*Oui.*" Daphne grinned like she was proud of herself.

Jared, who had just put the turkeys on the table, cut through the small crowd and put his hand on Sarah's lower back. "They are exquisite, Daphne. *Tres magnifique.*"

Daphne nodded her head up and down three times. "*Oui.*"

"But why?" Sarah asked. Confusion was knitting her brow and tangling her thoughts into knots she couldn't quite loosen.

"Effigies are French," Daphne said, surprising Sarah that she was speaking English. The entire room, which was now more than thirty people, gathered around as Daphne explained how when she learned about effigies, she realized it was one way she could honor the people in the town who made such a difference not only in the town itself but in her life.

Sarah interrupted, "But why place them anonymously here and there?"

"As little presents," she said. "Little surprises of joy." Her face glowed as she looked from person to person.

"So you meant no harm by them?" Chief James asked.

Daphne's face paled and she looked appalled. "*Non. Jamais.* I would never do such a thing."

"You're such an artist," Jared said. "The attention to detail has been astounding. I mean, look at the Whiskey effigy. It looks like you did every strand of fur separately."

Sarah looked at the miniature version of her dog that Daphne still held. Jared was correct. Threads of different shades created Whiskey's fur. This major detail brought tears to her eyes. The effigies were clearly a labor of love. She reached her hand out to Daphne, silently asking for the doll.

"*Oui,*" Daphne said, passing it to her. To Jared, she started talking about the different techniques she used to make each one, and as they launched in an art-making deep dive, people around them started filling their plates with food and sitting at the tables. The room was alive with the hum of conversations and silver clinking against plates.

Sarah found a spot next to Mrs. Jenkins, who leaned closer to her and said in Sarah's ear, "I think she's bored, dear. One can only shop online and study French so much to fill one's time."

Sarah eyed her neighbor, not sure where she was going with her comments. "Doesn't she work?" While Sarah had groomed Pierre and made small talk with Daphne for seven years, she suddenly realized she knew nothing about her, other than she had a killer wardrobe of high-end shoes and clothes.

"Not beyond managing her investments. Or maybe her family office does that," Janice said.

"Her family office?" Sarah didn't know what that meant.

"Yes, money managers for very high network individuals."

Sarah froze like a cat mid-pounce. "What!?"

"You've been reading about Cottageville history, Sarah. The Smith family was the most important in the founding of this town. Thomas Smith—"

Sarah finally caught on and interrupted, "Built the schools, the bank, the Methodist church, and a lot more."

"Yes," Mrs. Jenkins said. "Daphne's great-grandfather."

"But if she's so rich," Sarah asked, "why doesn't she go to France or any of or all of the places that speak French? Why does she never leave Cottageville?"

"Because sometimes we never overcome our childhood fears. Daphne's parents died in a plane crash. Her grandparents raised her and wouldn't fly after that and would never let her fly. Now she imposes that restriction on herself."

Sarah's mouth turned down. "That's so sad."

Mrs. Jenkins' patted her hand. "It is."

Sarah looked across the room at Jared and Daphne sitting together, Pierre on her lap. She looked down at the Whiskey effigy that sat above her plate. The little dog was so precise, so utterly Whiskey, it made Sarah's eyes tear.

She let out a long breath and then stood and turned to face the room. "First, I want to thank all of you for coming to our first Thanksgiving potluck." Fifty or sixty sets of eyes stared back at her. "It means so much to me to be a part of our town and for you to be a part of my life, well, mine, Jared, and Whiskey's. We love you, and we look forward to celebrating many more holidays with you."

From his seat near Daphne, Jared said, "And if there's any food leftover once everyone has had their fill, I'll have takeaway containers at the end of the table so you can have leftovers."

People laughed, applauded, and cheered.

Sarah's heart felt full...even fuller than her belly after she sampled each of the four different kinds of pies. She had solved Paul's murder, saved Bunky's life, and even discovered who had painstakingly made the effigies. Chief James stopped by on his way out the door to tell Sarah he'd return her and Jared's effigies to them tomorrow.

And at the end of the evening, Bill, Bunky, Janice, and Gladys had helped them clean up. The dishes had been washed and put away, all of the tables and chairs had been returned to their usual locations, and the buffet tables had been folded and stashed in a back room closet. The cafe was spotless and ready for business early the next day.

Sarah, Jared, and Whiskey parted with their friends and walked through the park toward their home. Jared and Sarah were holding hands and swinging their arms between them as they walked.

"What a great day," Sarah said.

"We have great friends and a really special community. Daphne has agreed to come to work with me part-time on books three and four. She's so talented, Sarah. I think she's just been wanting someone to appreciate it."

Sarah grinned at him. "And you do. Me too. I love you, J. Happy Thanksgiving."

"I'm grateful for you, my love." Jared placed a soft kiss on her lips.

Whiskey, who had been walking in front of them, stopped on the path and gave them a single "wuff," followed by his best black lip smile.

"We're grateful for you, too." Sarah told him, And she really was.

The End

JOIN US FOR WHISKEY DOG MYSTERY #7, RELEASING MARCH 1: *TULIPS, TAIL WAGS, AND THEFT*

Spring has arrived in Cottageville, Iowa, and dog groomer Sarah Carter is up to her elbows in fur and flower petals as the town prepares for its annual Tulip Festival. Between pet competition grooming and keeping her red heeler Whiskey out of the tulip beds, Sarah's schedule is full of sunshine and small-town charm—until the festival's prized golden tulip trophy vanishes.

When the artisan who created it disappears too, Sarah can't help sniffing around. But with jealous gardeners, rival shopkeepers, and more than one secret buried beneath Cottageville's perfect blooms, finding the culprit won't be easy.

With Whiskey's nose leading the way, Sarah digs into the mystery—one muddy paw print at a time. Because in Cottageville, even the prettiest gardens can hide the dirtiest secrets.

Learn about the latest releases and score free stuff by signing up for our newsletter.

Go to: https://www.whiskeydogmysteries.com and enter your email address at the bottom of the page to receive a free short story!